THE
WALKING
STONES

MOLLIE HUNTER

THE WALKING STONES

MAGIC CARPET BOOKS
HARCOURT BRACE & COMPANY
San Diego   New York   London

Requests for permission to make copies of any part of the
work should be mailed to: Permissions Department,
Harcourt Brace & Company, 6277 Sea Harbor Drive,
Orlando, Florida 32887-6777.

First Magic Carpet Books edition 1996
First published 1970 by Harper & Row

Magic Carpet Books is a trademark of
Harcourt Brace & Company.

Library of Congress Cataloging-in-Publication Data
Hunter, Mollie, 1922-
The walking stones/Mollie Hunter.
p.   cm.
"Magic Carpet Books."
Summary: After receiving the gift of Second Sight from
his old friend, the Bodach, ten-year-old Donald becomes
responsible for safeguarding the ancient power of the
walking stones before their glen is flooded by a
hydroelectric company.
ISBN 0-15-200995-7
[1. Supernatural—Fiction.   2. Friendship—Fiction.
3. Scotland—Fiction.]   I. Title.
PZ7.H9176Wal   1996
[Fic]—dc20   95-37916

Text set in Sabon
Designed by Trina Stahl
A C E D B
Printed in Hong Kong

This one for Rita,

with much thanks and love

CONTENTS

THE SECOND SIGHT

E LIVED IN a green glen deep among the mountains of the Scottish Highlands, and he was very old. That was how he came by the name of the Bodach, for in the Highlands there is an ancient language called Gaelic, and *bodach* is the Gaelic word for an old man.

This particular bodach was a fine man to look at, being very tall, with silky white hair that fell to his shoulders and a long beard of the same silky white. His features were big and strong, and brown with being out in all weathers, and although the blue of his eyes was faded, their look was kind, for he was a man of gentle nature. He was also a man who was greatly respected for his wisdom, and he had three possessions that were very precious to him.

One of these was a little old book of secret writings. Another was a rope of plaited cow hair, and the third was a tall staff made of bog oak, black in color and carved with many curious designs. The book and the rope he kept always in his little house in the glen, the book lying on the dresser in his kitchen and the rope hanging neatly coiled on a nail in the wall beside the kitchen fireplace. The staff, however, he carried with him wherever he went, and this was the most precious possession of all to him.

There was a river flowing through the glen where the Bodach lived, a deep and swift river with many streams running into it from the mountains on either side of the glen. The Bodach's house stood beside this river, and although it was only a small place of two rooms—a but-and-ben, as they call it—it suited him, since all he needed was a place to eat and sleep and keep his few precious possessions.

No one lived within miles of this but-and-ben except for a shepherd and his wife, Ian and Kitty Campbell by name, and their young son, Donald. This family, however, was company enough for the Bodach, and many a pleasant time he spent in their house. Indeed, he was like a grandfather to young Donald, who was just over ten years old at the time the things of which you shall hear began to happen, and the two of them were very fond of one another.

The Bodach, moreover, had the silver tongue of the born storyteller and Donald could never have enough of all the strange and wonderful tales he had to tell. The shepherd and his wife were also delighted to be so well entertained in such a lonely place, and so the Bodach was always a welcome visitor to the Campbells' house.

So it happened on an evening in January around two years ago that he had gone up the glen to spend an hour or two with these friends. Mrs. Campbell had made a baking of scones that day, and for a time they all enjoyed themselves, sitting around the fire drinking tea, eating scones, and listening to the Bodach telling stories from the long-and-long-ago times when all the best stories happened.

After a while, however, he fell silent and sat staring into the fire with a very thoughtful expression on his face. Ian Campbell and his wife had a quiet word or two with one another while they waited for him to come out of his dream, and the boy, Donald, sat hugging his knees as he watched the Bodach and thought to himself how white was the old fellow's long beard and how like the beak of an eagle was his great, bony nose.

Now it happened also that evening that all their conversation up to this point had been in English, but when the Bodach spoke again at last it was the old language—the Gaelic—that he used; and with his eyes still fixed on the glowing red of the fire and his tongue lingering over the music of this old language, he said slowly, "I see visitors coming to this house."

Donald and his parents turned to look toward the door of the house, expecting to hear a knock on it, but no knock came and in the silence that followed on the Bodach's words they suddenly remembered a certain strange power he was said to possess.

The Bodach, people said, was a man of the Second Sight, and by this they meant that he could see into the future and tell what would happen then—although this was not a power he could call up at will. Always it would come on him suddenly, without his expecting or desiring it. Then he would see a vision, as it were, of something that was still to be, and he would speak aloud of it as it took place before him.

This was what seemed to be happening to him now, for as he slowly lifted his gaze from the fire, they could see that his faded blue eyes had become as bright as glass and as blank as a mirror that has lost the power to reflect any image. His voice also, when he spoke again, had taken on a hollow, booming tone that was like the sound of a strong wind drumming in the darkness of a winter night; and still using the Gaelic, he went on in this hollow voice, "I see three men coming to this house, and these three men have but one name between them. The first of the three has hair like the white gold of the morning sun, and he carries a forest on his back. The second man has hair as red as sunset, and he carries lightning in his hand. The third man has hair as black as night. His hands are empty and he carries nothing on his back, but still he brings something to this glen. And the thing that he brings, is death."

The Bodach's voice broke off sharply on this last, terrible word, and he reached out his right hand, groping about with it like a blind man feeling for something. Mrs. Campbell shrank away from the touch of his groping fingers; and even young Donald, for all he was so fond of the Bodach, was a little afraid of him then.

Ian Campbell, however, was a strong man, as shepherds have to be, and not at all the kind of person to let fear master him. Moreover, he guessed what the Bodach's fingers were seeking, and so he rose to his feet and fetched the tall staff made of bog oak, black in color, and carved with many curious designs. He handed this to the Bodach and said firmly, "Can you tell us more about these three men? When will they come to the glen?"

"Tomorrow," the Bodach answered, and holding the staff upright before him, he gripped it with both his strong, old hands as if the feel of it was something his soul needed for comfort. "Tomorrow at this hour," he repeated, looking up at the shepherd with all the blank brightness suddenly gone from his eyes again. "That was all I saw, Ian lad, and that is all I can tell you."

Stiffly he raised himself from his chair by the fire until he stood his full tall height before them. His staff came up to his shoulder and it was very black against the smooth, shining white of his long beard. A look of great sadness he bent on them, standing thus, and in a voice that matched his look, he said, "Yet although I cannot see more, I greatly fear the outcome of it all. And so good night, my friends; and peace be on your house."

"Good night to you. And God go with you," the Campbells answered in chorus.

And so he left them, and went down the glen with a long, easy swing to his stride, while from the door they watched him and marveled to see such a bodach walking like a man still in his prime.

"A strange creature, the Bodach," Ian Campbell remarked when they were sitting around the fire again, "and there is a strange wisdom speaks out of him."

"Stuff and nonsense!" Mrs. Campbell said sharply. "And I wonder at you, Ian Campbell, for being so foolish as to encourage an old man's rambling talk."

"I only asked a question about his vision, Kitty," Ian Campbell protested. "There was no harm in that, surely!"

"Yes, there was," Mrs. Campbell insisted. "Vision, indeed! Who ever heard such rubbish in this day and age!"

Puzzled, the shepherd stared at her, and then he asked, "But, Kitty, do you not believe in marvels like the Second Sight?"

"Indeed, I do not," Mrs. Campbell retorted. "And I have no patience with people who believe such superstitious nonsense."

"That's as may be," the shepherd told her, "but I noticed it was enough to make *you* shiver at the time!"

"Aye," she agreed. "But who would not have shivered to see the uncanny look that was on the Bodach? Yet, still and all, my man, these are modern times, and the marvels *I* believe in are the modern ones I can see for myself—like television and airplanes. The Bodach will have to prove his marvel to me before I believe he can see into the future!"

So they argued about the Bodach, argued back and forth over young Donald's head, while he listened and wondered which of them had the truth of it. And all the time he listened he was seeing in his mind's eye a picture of three men, one with hair as white-gold as the morning sun, one as red as sunset, and one as dark as night. Yet his picture was not complete, for he could not imagine how any man could carry a forest on his back, or bring lightning to the glen; nor yet could he see how an empty-handed man could carry death with him.

Late, late that night, when he should have been asleep, Donald was still puzzling over these problems. And late, late also, the Bodach lay watching the moon painting yellow light on the one small window of his bedroom and thinking strange thoughts that would not let him rest.

When at last the Bodach could bear this uneasiness no longer, he got out of bed and dressed himself. The effort tired him, and sitting down on the edge of the bed again, he looked toward the corner where he had stood his tall staff. His hand came up, reaching out as if to grasp it, and as if his reaching hand had been a signal of command the staff came toward him.

Hop-hopping like a one-legged man, it crossed the space between them and stood upright before the Bodach. His fingers closed around it and he stood up briskly, as if he had somehow drawn new life from the feel of the staff in his hand; and moving not like an old man now but like a man in his prime, he left his house and strode off down the glen.

For a good half mile he walked, keeping close to the riverside all the time, and came to a halt at last where the river's uneven bank leveled out to make a flat, grassy space. There he stood, as still as stone himself, while he looked toward a ring of large stones that stood in the middle of this space.

There were thirteen of these stones, and they were all of the same shape. Each one was like a tall, flat pillar, two feet wide, six inches thick, and twelve feet high, and each one was spaced evenly apart from its neighbors. The ring they made was a huge and perfect circle that looked black against the moonlight, but the Bodach knew that daylight would show the color of the stones to be gray. He also knew that they were very old—older than the cleverest man in the land could guess or tell; and certain other things about them he knew, and meant to tell to young Donald Campbell someday, although this was a thought that was very far from his mind at that moment.

For a good while, then, he stood looking at the ring of stones. Then slowly he approached it, and slowly he walked to the center of the ring. When he reached what he judged to be this exact point, he placed his tall black staff upright upon it. Then he loosed his grip on the staff. It stood steady, without his needing to hold it in position, and he backed away from it until he was once more outside the Stone Circle. There he stopped, and from the space between two of the stones, he looked to see if anything was happening to the staff.

Almost immediately he noticed that it was quivering slightly. The quivering grew stronger until the staff began to vibrate back and forth, and the vibrations grew so rapid that his eye could not follow the motion. Then suddenly the vibrations stopped. The staff leaned outward from the point where he had placed it, and like a large minute hand circling the dial of a clock, it began to sweep around the circle of stones, pointing to them one by one.

Thirteen times it moved, and thirteen times it pointed before it returned to its upright position again. A moment only it stayed like this, then it swayed and fell, and the Bodach approached to pick it up.

Looking at it as he held it in his hand once more, he thought of his parting words to the Campbell family that evening—*I greatly fear the outcome of it.*

"And I was right to fear," he said aloud, "for now I know what that outcome will be."

And sighing deeply with the weight of that knowledge on him, he left the great circle of tall stones and put his foot to the road home.

2.

THE THREE RORYS

THE NEXT DAY was a school day for Donald Campbell, which meant that he had to rise very early, since there was no school nearer than the one in the village right at the foot of the glen. For Donald, this meant a two-mile walk down the riverbank to a point where there was a ford with big stepping-stones across it. Then once he had crossed the river, he had another two miles and a bit to walk to school.

All this was no bother to him as a rule, of course, he being an active country boy, born and bred to it; but on that particular

morning he was still tired after being awake
so long the previous night, and he set off
down the glen only half-hearing the message for the Bodach that his mother called
after him. By the time he got to the Bodach's house, however, he had managed to
shake himself awake, and remembering the
message, he hammered on the door.

From inside the house a voice called
sleepily, "Would that be yourself, Donald?"

"Aye," Donald called back, "and my
mother says, will you come to supper to-
night?"

"I will, and thank her kindly from me,"
came the answer, and Donald went on his
way wondering at an early riser like the
Bodach being so late abed on such a fine,
bright morning. He gave this no more than
a passing thought, however, for he had another thing to occupy his mind—or, to be
more exact, another person.

This other person was a boy called
Bocca, although Donald could not have
told you what or where that name came
from, any more than he could have told you
who or what Bocca was. All he knew was

that he had only to think of Bocca for
Bocca to be there beside him, and he was
quite content to leave matters at that, for
Bocca was the same age as himself and
liked the same kind of games. Moreover,
the long road to school would have seemed
even longer without him—especially then,
in winter, when the darkness came down
early and gave strange and sometimes
frightening shapes to quite ordinary things.

He was careful not to talk about Bocca
at home, however, because this only an-
noyed his parents. Bocca, they said, was not
a real person. Bocca, according to them,
was just someone Donald had invented
while he was still a very small boy and
lonely for a friend of his own age; but Donald did not believe this, for he could not
remember a time when he did not have
Bocca for a friend. Neither could he remember ever having invented him.

Yet still, he thought, his parents might
forbid him to play with Bocca altogether if
he argued the point, and so he never mentioned the name—except to the Bodach, of

course. The Bodach liked hearing about Bocca, and never argued about whether he was real or not.

"If he's real to you, Donald, then he is real," was all he ever said; and Bocca, running alongside Donald, was as real to him that morning as he was at any other time.

They played the kind of games they usually played together on the way to school—fighting imaginary battles with sticks for swords, jumping back and forward on the stepping-stones at the ford, and because it was still winter, cracking the ice that had formed in the shallows at the edge of the river. And as usual, of course, Donald was late for school as a result.

This meant he had to do a punishment exercise before he was free to leave school that afternoon, and what with that and dawdling again to play with Bocca on the road back from school, it was nearly suppertime before he finally reached home.

The kitchen was full of the warm smell of cooking when he came in, and his father was already back from work. The table was set for four people, and shortly after Donald's own return home, the Bodach arrived at the door.

"Come in, come in, man!" the shepherd invited. "I was telling the wife after you left last night that you would maybe like to be here this evening to see your three strangers when they arrive. And she said to me, 'Then what is to hinder him sitting down to supper with us first?' So here we are, all ready for you."

"Mistress Kitty has a kind heart, although she has a hard head," the Bodach answered, darting Mrs. Campbell a shrewd glance that told her he knew perfectly well what she thought of his "three strangers."

"Aye, maybe," she said, not wanting to discuss this with him, and then told them all to draw in their chairs. Her husband took the head of the table and asked a blessing on the meat, and then they all fell to the business of eating.

There was little talk as they ate, and even less when they had finished, for each one of them was secretly watching the hands of the kitchen clock creep around to the appointed hour of the strangers' visit. Yet even so, it was still a shock to them all when the expected knock came to the door, and Ian Campbell hesitated for a long moment before he rose to answer it.

The knock came again, and from outside the house a voice cried, "Is himself at home?"

"Yes, I am here," the shepherd called in reply, his voice a little hoarse with the uncertainty on him. He moved to the door and threw it wide. "Come in, gentlemen, and welcome to my house," he invited those beyond the door, and stood aside to let them enter.

There were three of them, just as the Bodach had said there would be. The first was a young man with a face that was smiling and kindly as well as handsome, and his hair was gleaming gold. The second man was middle-aged and rather stout, with a button nose and little blue eyes in a round face, and he had hair of fiery red. The third man, too, was middle-aged, with sharp unsmiling features, and his hair was deepest black; but the fair man had no forest on his back, the red one did not carry lightning, and there was no sign at all of the dark man's terrible burden—death.

The fair man, however, did have a large sack on his back, and while Donald stared in grievous disappointment for the lost marvels he had expected, the fair man swung his sack to the floor. Some pinecones spilled out of it, and seeing them, both Donald and his parents suddenly realized what the Bodach had meant when he spoke of a man carrying a forest on his back. For was there not a forest of trees all ready to grow from this great sack of seed?

The fair man saw the looks they gave one another, and quickly picking the pinecones up again, he said to Mrs. Campbell, "Excuse me, mistress, I was not meaning to make a mess of your nice clean floor."

"It's no matter, Mr.—Mr.—," Mrs. Campbell said nervously.

"Mackenzie," he told her, "Rory Mackenzie. But they call me Rory Ban, Rory the Fair, to mark me out from my two friends here."

He waved his hand to the other two, and the red-haired man stood forward.

"Rory Mackenzie is my name also," he explained, "but the color of my hair makes people call me Rory Ruadh, Red Rory."

"And I, too, am Rory Mackenzie," the dark man added, "and I am known as Rory Dubh, Black Rory."

Once again the three Campbells exchanged looks. Three men with but one name between them, the Bodach had said, and so here was another part of his vision coming true. Yet still, Donald thought, he could see no lightning in the hand of the red-haired man. There was nothing there except a roll of stiff blue paper, and pointing to this now, he told Rory Ruadh, "The Bodach said you would bring lightning to the glen, but you have brought nothing except that roll of paper."

Rory Ruadh turned a puzzled look on the Bodach, and Ian Campbell hurried to explain, "The Bodach here is a man of the Second Sight, and he foretold that you three would come here this evening."

"Did he now!" Rory Ruadh remarked, the puzzled look clearing off his face. "Tell me," he asked the Bodach, "was it in English or in the Gaelic that you told your vision of the Second Sight?"

"In the Gaelic, of course," the Bodach answered, "for that is the natural tongue of men of the Second Sight."

"True," Rory Ruadh agreed, "but it is not the tongue of modern science. Look!"

Quickly he spread out his roll of blue paper before them all. From end to end it was covered with a strange and complicated design traced in white, and pointing to this, Rory Ruadh told them, "There you see the plan of a hydroelectric power station that will soon be built in this glen, and so there you see also the explanation of what the Bodach saw in his vision."

"*I* did not see it!" said Donald, watching Rory Ruadh roll up the paper again.

"You see, do you not, that this thing in my hand brings electricity to the glen?" Rory Ruadh asked patiently.

"Aye," agreed Donald, "I see that."

"Well," said Rory Ruadh, "Gaelic is

such an old language that there is no word in it for modern things like electricity. But there is a Gaelic word for lightning, and so the Bodach used that word to tell what I would bring to the glen, for lightning is simply electricity in its natural form. Therefore, his vision was a true one—even though it was not the God-made lightning of the skies he saw in my hand, but the man-made lightning of my power station. Do you follow me, boy?"

"Aye," said Donald, "I can see it now!"

Then he looked at Rory Dubh, Black Rory. All the others followed his look, Red Rory and Rory the Fair included, and a chill little silence settled on the room.

In this little silence the Bodach said, "My vision told me that you would bring death to the glen, so answer me now, Rory Dubh Mackenzie. Did I see truly?"

"Yes," Rory Dubh told him quietly. "You saw truly."

"What form of death do you bring?" the Bodach asked then, and Rory Dubh answered, "The glen will be drowned."

"Drowned?" In a whisper, the shepherd

23

and his wife repeated the word, and Rory Dubh said, "Yes, I am sorry, but that is what will happen. The towns need more electricity, and using water power is the cheapest way to make it. That is why we must flood the glen."

"How will you do that?" Donald asked curiously.

"We will build a dam across the foot of the glen, and the water of the river will pile up behind that," Rory Dubh told him.

"But how can you use water to make electricity?" Donald wanted to know then.

Rory Ruadh stared at this, as if amazed that anyone could be so ignorant, but Rory Dubh went on, "You saw the plan of this power station we are going to build. Well, the dam will have openings, called sluices, in it, and these openings will have gates that can be raised or lowered so that we can control the flow of the water out of the glen. It will be a very powerful flow that will drop with great force to drive the turbines—the big machines that will be put into the powerhouse; and it is the turbines that will make the electricity."

"And I," said Rory Ruadh, looking important, "am the engineer in charge of *that* part of the work."

"And I," Rory Ban said with a smile, "am the forester who will plant trees to hide the scars the mountain will suffer while the dam is being built."

"And I," Rory Dubh finished soberly, "am the man who designed the dam and the power station, and who chose this site for them. I am the man charged with the building of them."

He looked at all their faces one by one. His own was stern, but not cruel, and they could see that he was not enjoying what he had to tell them.

"Remember," he said quietly, "my work will mean life to other people, though it means death to your glen. Also, it had to be built *somewhere,* and this is the most suitable site."

"But my house!" Mrs. Campbell cried. "My house will be drowned!" And she looked wildly around her kitchen, as if she could see the water coming in the walls at that moment.

"We will build you a new house in the village," Rory Ruadh told her. "A new, modern house with a refrigerator in it, and a washing machine, too."

Mrs. Campbell looked startled, and then pleased. "A washing machine!" she murmured to herself, beginning to smile, but now it was her husband's turn to object.

"What about my sheep?" he demanded. "What is to become of them?"

Rory Ban said, "I am afraid the trees and the water together will destroy the grazing, Mr. Campbell, but I can offer you a job as an assistant forester—a very well-paid job, with good holidays every year, and a bonus for every hundred trees planted."

"Well," said the shepherd. "Well!" And thought of all the years he had worked in all weathers with never a single holiday. "It sounds a good offer," he admitted.

"We hoped you would see it that way," Rory Dubh said. "That was why we decided to visit you and have a talk about the matter before you were given official notice to leave your home."

"Will my school be drowned, too?" Donald asked hopefully, but Rory Dubh shook his head.

"The dam will be built a little higher up the glen than where your school stands," he answered; and then, looking at the Bodach, he went on, "But this gentleman's house will be drowned and so he, too, will get a brand-new one in the village, with hot and cold running water in it, and fine big windows in place of the poky little ones he has now, and—"

"Enough!" the Bodach snapped, cutting across this speech. "I have heard enough talk about new houses for old!"

With dignity he rose to his feet, and stood there with his tall black staff planted firmly before him. His great height overtopped them all, his bushy white eyebrows were drawn down in a frowning glance that swept the three Rorys one by one, and in a voice that came up like a rumble of thunder from his chest, he said, "Now hear me, white son of the morning, red son of the evening, and dark son of night! The house I have now is my home, and I will not leave it except by my own choice. Therefore, build your power station and your dam if you like, *but you will never flood this glen until I give you leave to do so!*"

Turning on his heel then, he was at the door in three long strides, and there he swung around to look at them again. There was fire sparking from his faded blue eyes now. His head was held high, so that his eagle's beak of a nose jutted proudly as he raised his tall staff to point at the three Rorys, one after the other.

"Hear me," he repeated, "and be warned. For I have the power to do as I say I will do."

And with that he left them, striding off down the glen in lonely anger while the three Rorys turned puzzled looks on the shepherd and his wife.

"Did you ever hear talk the like of that?" Rory Ruadh exclaimed.

"He certainly spoke in a very odd way," Rory Ban agreed.

"It was all most unseemly," Rory Dubh said coldly.

"Ach, he was upset at the idea of having

to leave his house," Ian Campbell soothed them, and Mrs. Campbell added, "Old people do not like change, remember, and he is very old."

Donald Campbell said nothing at all, for he had something to think about that was even stranger than the Bodach's words—and that was the Bodach's staff. The Bodach had raised it to point at the three Rorys, but Donald was sure that he had seen no movement of the Bodach's hand *after* the staff was raised. It seemed to him, therefore, that the staff must have swung around of its own accord to point out each of the men in turn. Yet he could not understand how this could have been so, and he puzzled over it until the three Rorys' talking about the new dam distracted his attention again.

3.

THE TIGERS
AND BOCCA

IT WAS a week after the visit of the three Rorys that Ian Campbell got official notice of the plan to build the dam and the power station; and very imposing it looked, with HIGHLANDS HYDROELECTRIC BOARD printed in big blue letters across the top of it, and at the foot of the letter itself the signature of a man calling himself "the Secretary."

"Dear Mr. Campbell," this letter began, "It is with great concern for the welfare of you and your family that I have to inform you of a new hydroelectric program that will affect living conditions in your area."

"Look at that, how polite this secretary man is," said Ian Campbell approvingly as he read on from there. "I wonder, now, has the Bodach had the same kind of letter? And will that make him repent his stubborn words?"

The Bodach had, of course, received the same polite sort of letter from the secretary man, but it did not make the slightest bit of difference to him.

"Sell your sheep and go off to your new job in the forestry if you like," he said when Ian Campbell tried to reason with him, "but I will never leave this glen except of my own free will."

"Do you think they will let one old man hold up all this great new plan?" Mrs. Campbell raged at him. "They will *make* you leave your house. They will take you away and lock you up for the old madman you are!"

"They could do that, I suppose," the Bodach agreed. "But they will still not be able to flood the glen till I give them leave to do so."

"You are right, Kitty. He must be mad

to talk like that," the shepherd said later to his wife; and all anger gone now, she sighed, "Aye, God help him, for he must either be drowned along with his house or else taken from it by force, poor old soul!" And she wept for the Bodach, she having known him all her life and being fond of him for all she had scoffed at the notion of Second Sight and spoken hard words to him that day.

She was a pretty woman, Mistress Kitty, with the dark hair and dark blue eyes that are often seen among women in the Highlands, and she also had the rose-petal complexion that is their rare treasure; but now her eyes were all red with weeping and the tears were making blotches on her delicate skin.

Her husband tried to comfort her. Donald ran to put the kettle on, thinking that a cup of tea would steady her nerves, and while the kettle boiled he watched his father's strong brown face bent over his mother's fair, weeping one, and wondered what earthly reason the Bodach could have for being so stubborn. He could no more answer this question, however, than his parents could, and when word got about in the village of the new dam and the Bodach's threat to the three Rorys, the people there were every bit as puzzled as the Campbell family. The rest of that winter passed with much talk and guesswork on everyone's part, Donald's included, but when spring came all this was driven entirely out of his mind, for it was on a fine day in spring that the first of the tigers appeared in the glen.

They were the men who would build the dam, these tigers, and they had not been five minutes in the village at the foot of the glen before every boy in the school there knew that this is what dam builders are called. They came in bulldozers and Jeeps, big, tough-looking men wearing leather jackets and mud-stained trousers, with steel hats tilted jauntily on their heads, and boots laced knee high against the mud.

It was during the school lunch break they came, with Jeep horns blaring and amber warning lights flashing on the rooftops of the bulldozers' cabs, and when these machines growled to a halt, the boys swarmed like flies over them. The tigers swung down to the ground, stamping to take the cramp out of their booted legs and laughing at the boys' antics.

The biggest one of all among the men shouted, "Watch out for the tigers, boys!" and laughed to see them scatter before he told them what a tiger was.

Callum Mor, Big Callum, this man was called, and he was the chief man among the tigers. He was patient with the boys, however, and went to great trouble to answer all the questions they began to ask.

"The first thing we will do," he explained, "will be to build a road up to the site of the dam. We will need tons of rock to make a base for the road, of course, because it has to be strong enough to take the weight of all the heavy machinery we will be using; and that means we will have to blast the rock out of the mountainside with dynamite. So! Watch out for the red flags being posted, boys. They will be the signal to warn you when blasting is in progress."

Another spate of questions followed

then, and Callum Mor cried, "Hold your horses, boys! Give me a chance to explain!"

"Right, then," he went on when he had them all quiet, "this is how it will be done after the road is made. The next step will be to alter the course of the river so that it will flow away to one side of the dam site. This will leave us with dry land to one side of the glen and the river on the other. You follow me?"

"Yes, sir," the boys chorused.

"Right!" said Callum Mor. "Then we can begin digging out the foundations for the first part of the dam—the part that will be built across the river's old course. When we build this part of the dam, we will make sluices in it. These sluices are openings that can be closed or kept open as we choose, and so they will be our means of controlling the flow of water through the completed dam. Are you still following me?"

"Yes, sir," the boys chorused again.

And Callum Mor continued, "Very well, then. Our third step will be to direct the river back into its old course, which means it will then be flowing through the open sluices of the dam's first section. Are you still with me, boys?"

"Yes, sir!" the boys chorused louder than ever, and Callum Mor grinned all over his big red face.

"Aye, we'll make tigers of you all yet," he told them, and went on again, "We will build the powerhouse at the same time as we build the first half of the dam, of course, and after that the work will be a simple matter of extending the dam right across the width of the glen. *Now* let's hear your questions!"

"How will you change the course of the river?" one boy wanted to know.

"Easy!" Callum Mor answered. "We dig another channel for it, block up the old one with rocks and clay, and the river has no choice but to flow along this new channel. Then, when we want to bring it back to its old course, all we do is to remove the block from it and use the same material to close off the new channel!"

"How broad will the dam be?" Donald asked.

"Broad enough to take a road from one end of it to the other," Callum Mor told him.

"And how high?" came from another boy.

"A hundred feet," Callum Mor said, and all the boys gasped, telling one another in awed voices, "A hundred feet!"

"Ach, that's only a wee dam," one of the tigers said, grinning. "You should see some of the whoppers we've built in other glens!"

"Can we help with the building, sir?" a boy asked Callum Mor, but he shook his head at this.

"Why d'you think they call us tigers?" he asked. "No, my lad, you have to be big and strong, and a fierce fighter, too, before you conquer mountains and rivers as we do."

That was the end of it, for the bell to call them back into school rang just then, and the boys jostled their way through the school door, each boasting that he would be first on the site of the road-making the next day, and each trying to shout down his neighbor's boast.

37

By the time they came out of school, however, the tigers had already run power lines into the village. Some of them were busy assembling living quarters for the squad, from the truckloads of housing units that had arrived. There were two bulldozers at work, shearing their way through tons of rock and earth and leaving a flattened trail behind them; and from the camp to the hillside, where other tigers were blasting rock to make bottoming for the new road, there stretched a line of flags flying red for danger.

With yells and whoops of excitement, the boys rushed to watch the work—and that was the beginning of dam fever among them!

From first peep of light in the morning to last thing at night, after that day, you could see boys scrambling to get as near as Callum Mor would allow them to the site of the dam, each one secretly hoping to get a shot at driving a bulldozer or a Jeep.

They badgered their mothers to buy them steel helmets and high-laced boots like those worn by the tigers. They copied the way the tigers walked and the way they talked. They ran errands for them, and brought them billy-cans of tea, hot and strong and sweet, for there was not a single one of them now but longed to be a tiger himself someday.

Callum Mor was their hero in all this, and when Rory Ruadh drove up in his Jeep to inspect the work they would shout a greeting to him, just as Callum Mor did; and Rory Ruadh, being a friendly, easy-going man, would shout back as cheerfully at them. Rory Dubh was a different case, however. He had a very forbidding look about him, and moreover, he was the real boss of the whole operation. Callum Mor always saluted respectfully when he appeared, and the boys did the same, standing up straight and touching their hats to this dark, unsmiling man.

As for Rory Ban, no one except Donald Campbell ever saw him, since he was always working in his nursery of seedling trees on the high slopes of the upper part of the glen.

Even Donald, however, never caught

more than a glimpse of him, for Donald was as mad with dam fever as the rest of the boys. Every morning for the rest of that spring, and for the whole of that year's summer and autumn, he left the house at a run and sped as fast as he could down the glen to the site of the dam; and every evening he lingered to watch the work until darkness put an end to it for the day.

There was never any dawdling for him now on the way back and forth to school, and that meant, of course, that there was no time either for the company of his friend Bocca. Donald did not miss Bocca, however, since his mind was so full of other things that he had no need of company; and because Bocca was never there except by Donald's own wish, the months sped quite happily past without a sign of him.

As for the Bodach, it was little enough that Donald saw of him then either, the long light evenings of summer not being the time for sitting around the fire listening to stories; and never for a minute did Donald dream that a day would come when both Bocca and the Bodach would be brought suddenly and very sharply to his attention again. Nor could he ever have imagined the strange way in which this would take place!

All unsuspecting, therefore, he got ready to go with his father one day in late autumn when he was told he must help to search for a sheep that had strayed. It would be no hardship, he thought, to miss one day at the dam now, for with the summer holidays behind him he had been able to watch the tigers for weeks on end; and so he set off cheerfully beside his father with the collie dogs, Nip and Tuck, running at their heels.

It was to the low slopes of the mountain they were headed, to the grazing ground where the rest of the flock was pastured. Once there they separated, each taking a dog to help him in the search. Donald took Nip with him, and his father took Tuck, yet search as they would, neither of the dogs had got so much as a sniff of the lost sheep by the time they all met again.

"The silly thing has maybe got itself trapped on a ledge of rock higher up the mountain," Mr. Campbell said. "You take that eastward path, Donald, and go on straight up the mountain. I'll take the dogs and make a wider cast to the west, and we'll meet again at the top."

So they parted once again, and Donald set his foot to the trail, quite well pleased with his share in this part of the search, since he always enjoyed climbing straight up a mountain and seeing the world grow small beneath him as he went. Also, there was something about the atmosphere of a mountaintop that had always had a powerful attraction for him.

He liked the silence that was there, and the stillness that mountain air has when the weather is fine, for it was not a dead stillness. There was something living at the heart of it—something he sensed in the same way a dog can sense a sound that is too far away or too high pitched for human ears to hear—and this something gave him the strangest feeling that the mountain itself must be alive.

And all the other mountains he could see as he climbed—they were alive too! He could feel that they were watching him, like great heads staring down from a wide and private world slung halfway between sky and earth; yet watching in a friendly manner, as if encouraging him to mount on and up into the great and living stillness of that world.

And so on he would go, half-curious and half-afraid, yet always with a great excitement on him, till he had reached the top at last; and there he would stay for a long time, listening, listening to the silence, and trying hard to hear the living something at the heart of it.

He had never quite succeeded in doing so, of course, but he was quite sure that he would someday, and this was the great attraction that mountains had for him. Yet mountains have their dangers as well as their attractions, and on the Scottish mountains especially, there is a kind of danger that frightens even experienced climbers and takes the lives of many who go out unprepared for it.

Suddenly, they find—so suddenly that there seems to be no warning at all of its happening—a dense mist will come down on the mountaintop or will rush upward in great smoky columns from the glen below. And there they are, trapped, not able to see more than a foot ahead, and in the blink of an eye the peaceful mountainside has become a death trap of hidden ledges and sheer drops down to eternity.

This danger, then, was the one that lay in wait for Donald as he climbed upward in search of the sheep that day. One instant the glen below him was clear and sunny. The next it was filled with great swirls of mist rushing upward to smother him the way a breaking wave smothers a pebble on the shore.

Yet he did not panic when this happened, for being mountain born and bred he knew that the secret of safety lay in keeping perfectly still until the mist had dispersed again. Also, he guessed that if this took too long to happen, his father would send Nip and Tuck to find him and the dogs would lead him safely back down the mountainside.

He settled himself patiently to wait, therefore, although the mist was cold and he wished he had brought a jacket with him. Waiting was lonely work, too, and he began to feel very downhearted after a while. It was then, for the first time in months, that he thought of Bocca and longed to have him there for company; but it was only a few seconds after this that the mist began to clear so that he could see the shoulder of the mountain rising above him again.

As it came into view once more, he saw also, with some surprise, that there was someone standing there looking down into the mist-filled glen below. When the mist cleared still further, he realized it was the Bodach who was standing there, and that the place toward which he was gazing was the site of the construction work on the dam. He opened his mouth to shout to the Bodach, but before he could get the words out he suddenly became aware of Bocca standing by his side.

It was an awkward moment for Donald, he having neglected Bocca for so long. Surprise, also, robbed him of speech; and he was still trying to recover his wits when Bocca began walking away from him and

45

toward the Bodach. Bocca reached the
Bodach, and the two of them stood side by
side for a moment, the thin swirls of mist
around them making them seem like darker
shapes of mist themselves. Then slowly they
walked off together, mist figures vanishing
into denser mist, leaving Donald wondering
if he had imagined the whole thing.

Or was it only Bocca he had imagined?
The Bodach was a real person, after all, but
his parents had always said that Bocca was
just a creature of his own imagination, and
now, Donald thought, it looked as if they
had been right all along! He had been
lonely standing there in the mist by himself,
and so he had simply imagined Bocca had
appeared to keep him company. But if that
was true, then that was also the way it had
always been. He had imagined Bocca from
the very beginning, just because he had
been lonely for a friend of his own age.

Far below him, Donald heard Nip and
Tuck barking hoarsely. He whistled to let
them know where he was, and as they came
searching up the mountainside with his
father's voice urging, *"Seek, Nip! Seek,*

Tuck!" he recalled something about the appearance of the Bodach as he stood there on the shoulder of the mountain.

He had not been carrying his tall staff, and this was very puzzling, for the staff was as much a part of the Bodach as his own right arm. He never went abroad without it—never! It was odd, Donald thought, very odd indeed; and the sight of these two misty figures vanishing into the mist had been an eerie one.

A little chill that was not caused by the coldness of the mist passed over him. He began to shiver, and although it was only a few minutes afterward that his father arrived with the dogs, it seemed a very long time to him.

Nip and Tuck leaped up, hurling their warm, furry bodies against him. Warm, too, was his father's arm lying across his shoulders—a real flesh-and-blood arm, Donald thought thankfully, not imagination, as Bocca had been; and through chattering teeth he said, "Dad, you were right about Bocca. I only imagined him."

"Aye, then!" his father said, laughing,

"and what thoughts have you had up here to bring you to your senses about that, eh?"

"Well—" Donald thought for a bit and then decided it would be altogether too difficult to describe what he had been thinking.

"I just decided, that's all," he said at last, and his father told him, "Good lad, Donald. You're beginning to grow up!"

And so they went down the mountainside together to continue their search, and not long afterward they came on the lost sheep stuck in a patch of boggy ground and half-dead with struggling to free itself. Between them, they brought it to safety; yet all the time this was going on Donald still could not help puzzling over the question of the Bodach and his staff—for he *had* seen the Bodach. That was one thing he had not imagined up there. And there *had* been something oddly different about him then—in fact, Donald thought suddenly, it had almost seemed as if the Bodach with his staff and the Bodach without his staff were two separate persons!

It was thinking like this that made him

remember how mysteriously the Bodach's staff had seemed to turn of its own accord in his hand when he raised it to point at the three Rorys; and coming together in his mind like this, the two things decided him.

Someday when he had the chance, he thought, he would speak to the Bodach about his staff, and if there was some kind of mystery about it, he would find out the nature of that mystery!

4.

WINTER'S TALES

T WAS just over a year from the time of Donald's strange experience on the mountain that the Campbell family moved into the new house that had been built for them in the village, and during that time there was a lot of work done on the dam.

The tigers finished the first section of it—the section in which they had made the sluices that would control the flow of the water when all the work was completed. Into this section also they built the power-house that looked for all the world like a great square fort standing on guard at one end of the dam.

Now was the time for Rory Ruadh to set about installing the great turbines that were to make the electricity, and as the second summer of the dam building came around he was in the powerhouse every day, directing this work. By the end of that summer the tigers had finished the work of diverting the river back into its former course, so that now it ran through the sluices in the dam's first section. This left them with a clear field for working on the dam's second and final section, and it was when they started on this that the Campbells moved into their new house.

Now Donald could spend as much time as he liked at the dam, and so he was delighted with the move. Mrs. Campbell was charmed by her new house, which had central heating in it, electric light, hot and cold running water, an electric stove, a refrigerator, and a washing machine—everything, in fact, that a modern house should have—and daily she gave thanks that she would never have to trim a paraffin lamp again, or stoke a peat fire, or carry buckets of water from the river for her washing.

As for Ian Campbell, he found that he enjoyed working in the tree nursery with Rory Ban, who, he said, had green fingers on either hand and was a very pleasant young fellow as well. Nor did he mind very much about having to sell his sheep, since he got a good price for them and the life of a shepherd is a hard one at the best of times.

He kept the dogs, Nip and Tuck, however, not liking to part with such old friends; and they were company for Donald whenever he went back up the glen to visit the Bodach—for the Bodach, of course, had not moved to the village.

There was a new house waiting there for him, every bit as modern as the one the Campbells had, yet still he clung to his old but-and-ben by the river and nothing that anyone said could persuade him to leave it—not any warnings from the three Rorys, nor any arguments from Ian Campbell, nor yet any pleading from Mrs. Campbell.

The Bodach listened to all they had to say, looking steadily at them from under his bushy white eyebrows as they spoke. But never a word would he say in reply except, "I am staying here till I am ready to leave." And never a hint would he give them of when that would be.

"I just do not know what to make of him," sighed Rory Ban, who had formed quite a friendship with the Bodach during that first summer of the dam building, when he had worked all alone in his tree nursery.

"He is crazy—soft in the head," said Rory Ruadh and Rory Dubh, echoing what Mrs. Campbell had already said about the Bodach.

Yet still she and her husband felt sorry for the Bodach, living up there all alone. Also, in spite of the entertainment they got out of their new television set, they found that they missed him, for there was no one on television who knew stories as strange as the ones he told, or who could tell them half so well.

Donald, however, had no such regrets, for when he lived in the old house it had been his habit to carry the Bodach's weekly basket of groceries home to him from the village, and even after the move he kept up with this habit. Every Friday after school he collected the groceries from Kenny the Shop, the owner of the store. Then, with a basket of his mother's baking on his other arm and Nip and Tuck running at his heels, he set off on his weekly visit to the Bodach.

This was time away from the dam that he never grudged, since it was a trip that he liked making—and for more than one reason. First of all, there was the warm welcome he always got from the Bodach, then there was the cup of tea always waiting for him beside the peat fire on the hearth, and a share in the good things his mother had sent to go with it.

"There's nothing to beat this, eh, Donald?" said the Bodach the first time they sat together like this, drinking tea and eating buttered scones; and Donald was inclined to believe him. Outside, the autumn air already had a nip of frost in it, and although his own house was warm enough, central heating was nothing like so cheerful as the red glow of this good peat fire. The Bodach had drawn the curtains against the night coming down, and the paraffin lamp on the dresser was casting a soft yellow glow over the room.

Donald looked at the lamp, comparing it with the bright electric light in his new home, and he said, "Your lamp is not near so bright as the light we have nowadays."

"No," the Bodach agreed, "it makes shadows in the room, but a soft light is kind to the eyes, and forbye, shadows are good for the imagination."

"That's true," Donald agreed, and then he said, "We have television in our new house."

"D'ye tell me that!" the Bodach exclaimed. "I wonder now, Donald, did you ever see on this television of yours the story of the giant with the two heads that kept quarreling with one another?"

"No, I never did," Donald told him, and the Bodach said, "Well, then, maybe they would be telling the tale of the Great Gray Man that haunts the slopes of Ben Mac-Dhui?"

"No, they would not," said Donald, and the Bodach exclaimed, "Dear, oh dearie me! Would they be telling, then, the story of the Great Stones?"

"You know fine they wouldn't," Donald said. "There's no one but yourself knows stories like that—and what Great Stones are these, anyway?"

"The ones down the glen, of course," the Bodach told him. "The Stone Circle you used to pass every morning on your way to school. Once every hundred years, they say, these stones move from their places. They walk to the river and dip their heads in it, then they go back to their places and stand fast there for another hundred years."

"I would only believe that if I saw it for myself," Donald said.

"Other people have said the same," the Bodach remarked. "They have gone to watch for the stones moving on the night it was supposed to happen, and in the morning they have been found lying beside the stones—dead."

A little impressed in spite of himself,

Donald asked, "And is that the whole story of the stones?"

The Bodach slid him a sidelong glance. "No," he said quietly, "there is more to it than that; but only for some people. Someday, maybe, I will tell you the rest of it, for I think you may be one of those people. But only maybe, and only when I think the time is right to tell it."

"Och, well then," said Donald, a bit disappointed, "tell me another story. Tell me about the two-headed giant."

"Oh, him." The Bodach smiled. "He was a most misfortunate man, that giant! You see, Donald, it was like this—"

And that was the Bodach fairly launched into a whole evening of tale telling, which was the thing Donald had always enjoyed most about his company. It was also, of course, the chief reason for his liking of the weekly trip up the glen, for no one who has been charmed by the silver tongue of the born storyteller is ever truly released from its spell; and Donald, you must remember, had been under that spell all his life.

Many of the Bodach's stories he had heard before, of course, but always there was a different one if he wanted it—maybe a tale of old, brave battles with the sound of trumpets still ringing in it; or maybe one of fair, dead heroes that was sad as the whispered sea sorrow of small waves lapping a deserted shore.

Sometimes, also, the Bodach told tales of knaves defeated and rogues confounded, and these he told with a quick, dry wit, yet with such a face of innocence on him that his very look was enough to set Donald rocking with laughter.

But of all the stories the Bodach told, Donald's favorites were always those that spoke of the strange, shadowy beings of the Otherworld—the world of seal-men, kelpies, urisks, and all the other creatures of Highland legend; the world where sea sands could sing, where peerie-men and trolls could be heard hammering away inside the hollow hills, and where witches could, for their sins, be changed into the shape of great gray mountain peaks and stay frozen like that for all eternity.

"Like the Five Sisters of Kintail," the Bodach told him. "Five witches they were once, but now they are the five mountains that brood over the glen called Glen Shiel, and when the mist boils up thick and gray like smoke around them, people still say, 'Ah, the Sisters are boiling up their witches' cauldron again!' "

It was just about time for Donald to go home on the evening the Bodach told him this, and since they had fallen into the habit of meeting at the ford and walking back there together also, the Bodach reached for his staff as he spoke. His words and the gesture coming together reminded Donald of the questions he had put to himself that day he had been trapped on the mountainside by the mist, and he wondered if the time was ripe to ask them now.

So often before this, he thought, the questions had been on the tip of his tongue to ask, but somehow he had never managed to find the right words for them!

"Ready, Donald?" the Bodach asked.

"Aye," Donald answered, and made up his mind on the word. Like a true Highlander, however, he took care not to give offense by coming directly up to the subject, but edged up to it sideways, as it were.

"That's surely a fine staff you have there," said he, as they made for the door together. "Would you have a story about it, too, by any chance?"

The Bodach shot him a look that was, as they say, old-fashioned. "Aye," he said. "There is a story about my staff, but I will tell it to you only when I tell you the story of the Stone Circle—if I ever do tell you that story." And he shot Donald another look that dared him to say one word more on the subject.

"Yes, sir," said Donald, knowing when he was beaten. The Bodach and he were friends, and next to his parents there was no one who meant more to him. Yet still he stood in awe of the Bodach when that particular look was in his eye, and so they walked together to the ford talking of other things.

That was the way of it, then, between Donald and the Bodach all that second winter of the dam building; and Donald never bothered about the darkness of the long road he had to travel on his visits, since he always had the Bodach's company to and from the ford. Then, once they had parted there, he had Nip and Tuck to trot before him the rest of the way home, and the white undersides of their tails made markers that guided him through the darkness.

There were occasions, too, when he had Rory Ban's company on his Friday trips, for the way of Rory Ban's friendship with the Bodach was this: The Bodach nearly always had some wild creature in his care that had been given to him by Rory Ban.

It was one of the sad things about a forester's work, as Rory Ban explained to Donald, that very often the homes of such creatures were destroyed when the ground was cleared for planting of the new trees, and if they were too young to find their own food he could not endure to see them die of starvation; nor did he have the heart to kill any of those that were wounded in the course of this planting work.

The Bodach, however, had come to his aid in this, he having a natural talent for handling wild creatures. Those too young to fend for themselves he would feed till they were old enough to seek their own food; the wounded ones he would doctor and tend till they were well again; and it was partly to visit these creatures and partly because he had grown to like the Bodach for his own sake that Rory Ban sometimes seized the chance of going up the glen with Donald.

Nor did Donald mind this—in fact, he welcomed the company of such a quiet, pleasant man as Rory Ban. He was pleased, also, to find that at least one of the Rorys had found the true worth of the Bodach, for several times as they walked home Rory Ban said to him, "There is a great deal more to the Bodach than meets the eye, Donald. You are lucky to have him for a friend."

"Aye, he's good company," Donald agreed, thinking at the same time that he could truthfully pay this compliment to Rory Ban also, for his talk about forestry was always very interesting, and he seemed to enjoy the Bodach's stories as much as Donald did himself.

Thus, when there were the three of them, the Friday evenings passed as pleasantly as at other times, with Nip and Tuck curled at their feet and the bright eyes of some of the Bodach's nurslings watching from some shadowed corner while the firelight toasted their faces and Rory Ban's fair, bright head shone even brighter gold in the soft yellow lamplight enclosing them.

The sound of the Bodach's voice was the spell that held them all peaceful and silent then, but there was talk also, between one story and another, since Donald always had news of home and the village to bring, and Rory Ban always liked to inquire after his creatures and to give the Bodach the latest news of his forestry work. Many other things that were neither here nor there they talked of also, but the one thing that was never mentioned was the work on the dam, the Bodach having made it quite clear he did not want to discuss it and the other two being happy to abide by this.

That work was going forward all the same, however, and as winter turned into spring again there came a time when

Donald forgot the rule not to mention it in the Bodach's presence. It was while he and Rory Ban were walking up from the ford with the Bodach one evening that it happened, and it was a remark by the Bodach himself that set him off.

"It's growing weather again—look!" said the Bodach, pointing his staff to a clump of primroses.

"Aye, and building weather, too," Donald answered without thinking. "It will not be long now before the dam is finished. They have even set a date for the flooding of the glen—the twenty-third of April, it is, and my mother says she read in the papers there is to be a great ceremony to mark the occasion."

"I read that, too," Rory Ban said, laughing. "There is to be Royalty there, no less, and she pushing a golden switch with the fingertip of her white glove to set the whole thing in motion!"

"And a brass band, my mother says," Donald added, warming to his theme. "And balloons and streamers, and flags for all the children."

"And I've no doubt," said the Bodach, smiling in his beard, "that Inverness Town Council is going to be there, and all the Town Councillors dressed up in their scarlet and ermine robes! *And* the Lord Lieutenant of the County! *And* the Chairman of the Hydro Board! *And* the Chief Constable!"

Surprised, because he knew the Bodach never bothered with newspapers, Donald said, "Yes, they will be—but how did you know?"

"Because I know the way people think," the Bodach retorted, and Rory Ban said, "That's right, Donald. They all think there's no show without Punch!"

"Well, they need not bother coming to see this show," the Bodach told him, "for it will never take place."

Donald and Rory Ban exchanged looks, and then Rory Ban said gently, "They are bound to succeed in the end, you know, even if you do stop them flooding the glen this time."

"I have never said I wanted to hold out against them forever," the Bodach pointed out. "All I said was that they could not flood the glen till I gave them leave to do so; and I will not give them that leave till my purpose in staying here has been fulfilled."

What that purpose was, however, he still would not say, and there was no further talk of the dam until Donald and Rory Ban were going home together that evening. It was Donald again who brought up the subject then, and this time it was in the form of a question.

"Rory Ban," he asked, "do you think the Bodach really has the power to stop the glen being flooded?"

Rory Ban took time to consider this, and then he answered, "He has power of some kind, Donald; of that I am certain. But as for how he means to use it, I know no more than you do."

They walked in silence for a while longer, and then Rory Ban said, "I'll tell you something, Donald. I have been watching you this past winter, sitting there in the Bodach's house, and you drinking in all the stories he has to tell you. I have been watching him, too, as he told these stories, and more than once it has struck me that you are like teacher and pupil together—he the master of a strange wisdom, and you the willing student of that wisdom."

"Aye, you could say that," Donald agreed. "I have learned a lot from the Bodach's stories."

"And such learning is not to be had in the schools," Rory Ban said soberly, "for it seems to me, Donald, that the Bodach's wisdom is not entirely of this world. There is something in it of the Otherworld he talks of in his stories, and I have the feeling that he is as much at home there as he is in this ordinary world of ours."

"I am not so sure, then, that I want to be wise in the way the Bodach is wise," Donald said uneasily. "It is maybe not a good thing, after all, for me to be learning so much from him."

"Nonsense!" Rory Ban exclaimed. "You are twelve years old now, Donald. That is old enough to know that the Bodach's teaching is good because his heart is good, and my advice to you is to learn all that you can from him. There are not many of his kind left in the world—more's the pity—and it's you should be happy to have the chance of learning from him."

"I would be happier still," said Donald, "if I could learn how he means to stop Rory Dubh from flooding the glen."

"Then want must be your master," retorted Rory Ban, "the same as it must be for all of us until the twenty-third of April. And then we might all learn quick enough what his powers are!"

5.

THE BODACH AND
THE DAM

APRIL THE 23rd was a Saturday. It was also a fine, clear day, and the sun was shining brightly at nine o'clock that morning, when Rory Dubh sent Callum Mor up the glen with three of his tigers.

Their orders were plain. They were to tell the Bodach once again that the flooding of the glen would surely drown him if he insisted on staying where he was, and they were to ask him to come quietly back down the glen with them. If he would not come quietly, Rory Dubh had warned, they were to take him by force; and being decent men at heart, the tigers did not like this part of their orders at all. They were most relieved, therefore, when the Bodach made no argument but simply picked up his staff and walked peaceably with them back to the foot of the glen.

There was a great crowd of people already assembled by the time they arrived there, and the larger part of these were seated on the slope of the mountain overlooking the dam site, like people sitting in the gallery of a theater waiting for the play to begin. The road running across the top of the dam was also crowded with spectators, since all the employees of the Hydroelectric Board had been given tickets for themselves and their families to view the ceremony from this privileged position.

The Bodach stopped to look at this scene, his gaze taking in both the green sweep of the mountainside and the dazzling white of the hundred-foot-high wall of the dam. There was a parapet edging both sides of the road across it, and he smiled to see the row of heads craning down from the parapet edge that faced up the glen.

"Are my friends the Campbells up there?" he asked, and Callum Mor told him, "Aye, they are there with their laddie and Rory Ban—beside the control cabin, there."

He pointed up to the small, square cabin that was set into the center of the parapet above them, and that housed the switches controlling the opening and closing of the gates for the sluices. The Bodach smiled again.

"They will get a good view from there," he remarked. "But where is my place to be?"

"On the slope of the mountain there," Callum Mor told him, "just where Constable MacDonald is standing."

"So that he can keep an eye on me, eh?" the Bodach said, smiling.

"You could put it that way," Callum Mor admitted uncomfortably, and he led on toward Constable MacDonald, who was one of a number of policemen helping to keep order among the crowd on the mountainside.

There they left the Bodach, seated

among the other spectators, and hardly settled in his place before the children around him were asking for a story. "And not a word of protest out of him from first to last," as Callum Mor said, turning away from passing on the orders he had been given for the constable.

And hurrying alongside him as he went back to the dam to make his report to Rory Dubh, the tigers agreed, "Aye, it seems a proper shame to treat such a harmless old man so like a criminal."

Nor were Callum Mor and his tigers the only ones to have such thoughts, for the Campbells and Rory Ban had a good, all-around view from their position on the dam, and they had seen all this happening.

"It seems to me that Rory Dubh is making a great fuss over nothing," Ian Campbell remarked, and Mrs. Campbell added indignantly, "Forbye, he has no right to put a great big policeman to watch over the Bodach as if he was some kind of low-down rascal instead of a good-living old man!"

"It's only for his own good," Rory Ban

consoled her. Then he glanced at Donald, as if asking him what he thought of this turn of events, and said in a low voice, "There's no way he can stop the flooding now."

Donald stood silent, not knowing whether to be relieved or disappointed at the way things were turning out. After all, he thought, he was not really sure that he wanted the glen to be flooded, for that would mean the end of the place where he had lived all his life! And he was sorry for the Bodach, of course; besides which, it was a bit disappointing to think he would not get the chance to find out if the Bodach really did have the power to stop the flooding. But then again, all the great work of building that had entertained him so much had been done just for that purpose, and the great waves of water that would spread out to cover the glen once the sluice gates were closed would certainly be a fine sight to see!

"I don't know, Rory Ban," he said at last, sighing. "Maybe it's just as well things are as they are." And trying not to think any more about it, he went back to watching all the fuss that was going on in the village beyond the dam.

Twelve o'clock was the time set for the ceremony of moving the switch that would flood the glen, and it lacked an hour yet to that time, but already the school playground was nearly full with cars and buses parked there for the occasion. Another bus drove up, and out came the band in blue-and-silver uniforms, with their trumpets and horns and trombones glittering gold in the sun.

The schoolchildren lined up at the front of the crowd on the mountainside cheered and waved their flags when they saw the band arrive. The bandsmen trooped up the steps leading to the road on top of the dam and formed up in two lines against either side of the parapet. The conductor raised his baton. The band burst out with "Scotland the Brave," and all the children cheered and waved their flags again in time to the music.

Then along came the great, sleek, black

car that carried the Lord Lieutenant of the County, and he stalked onto the dam, looking very grand in a cocked hat, with a sword at his side and golden epaulettes on the shoulders of his red uniform jacket. Behind the Lord Lieutenant walked a few Dukes and Duchesses, and some Lords and Ladies who had also got themselves invited to the show, and all these people came to stand near Rory Ban and the Campbells.

"It won't be long now," said Ian Campbell, pointing out the Chief Constable standing all ready to open the door of Royalty's car.

But it was Town Councillors who were in the next lot of cars to arrive.

Walking two by two, and headed by the Lord Provost with his golden chain of office shining brightly on his chest, they came up on to the dam, tripping a bit over their long red robes as they mounted the steps and sweating more than a bit in the warmth of their fur collars and white gloves. They looked very dignified in spite of that, however; but since most of them were fat men there was not much room for anyone else once they had taken up their positions on the dam.

It was only around the control cabin that there was a little clear space left, for it was beside the other switches inside the cabin that the golden switch had been placed—the one that Royalty's white-gloved finger would push to start them all working. And that was the moment that everyone was waiting for now.

Rory Ruadh and Rory Dubh were both standing ready beside the control cabin. They had been as nervous as cats until Callum Mor had come up on the dam to make his report to them, but with just over half an hour to go now before the great moment arrived and everything in good order, they were looking like the same cats that had just had cream.

Rory Ruadh strolled over to where Rory Ban and the Campbells were standing beside the parapet overlooking the glen and said cheerfully, "Well, now. It seems there has been a lot of fuss for nothing over the Bodach, eh?"

Mrs. Campbell, who was still feeling put out over the way the Bodach had been treated, said sharply, "You have made sure of that, Rory Ruadh."

"*I* made sure of it, ma'am," said Rory Dubh, coming forward to join their group. "But this is a big and expensive project, you know, and I could not afford to take any chances."

"Ach, for all the difference the Bodach could have made to your fine big project!" Mrs. Campbell said scornfully, and Donald turned away from the argument, wondering which of them had the truth about the Bodach. Had it been harsh of Rory Dubh to set a policeman to watch him—or had it been wise?

Leaning his elbows on the parapet while he thought about this, he stared down into the glen and was puzzled to see the policeman who had been watching the Bodach running down toward the foot of the dam. The policeman was pointing and shouting as he ran; and looking to where he pointed, Donald saw the Bodach standing on the riverbank, waving his arms up to the people

77

on the parapet as if to say, *I am here! Do you not see? I am here! Here!*

Such a shock of surprise this was to Donald that his breath left him for the moment, but he recovered as quickly again, and jogging Rory Ban's arm, he said urgently, "Look down there, Rory Ban! It's the Bodach—do you see him?"

Rory Ban looked and saw the Bodach. "You're right!" he exclaimed, surprised in his turn, and turning his head back over his shoulder, he shouted, "Hey, Rory Dubh! Look down here—the Bodach has escaped from the policeman you set to watch him!"

Rory Dubh rushed to look over the parapet. Rory Ruadh and Callum Mor crowded behind him, and Rory Ruadh said angrily, "What on earth does the old fool mean by all that shouting and waving? It will spoil the ceremony to have him carrying on like that when everyone is supposed to be attending to the royal speech."

"He won't get the chance to spoil anything," snapped Rory Dubh, and with a grim look on his face he dashed into the control cabin and began calling over the mi-

crophone there, "Chief Engineer to Chief
Constable . . . Chief Engineer to Chief Constable. There is a trespasser on the scene of
operations. Arrest him . . . Arrest him . . ."

Rory Ruadh and Callum Mor began
quarreling with one another as the message
went out, Rory Ruadh blaming Callum
Mor for not having made sure of a better
guard being kept on the Bodach, while Callum Mor kept asking angrily, "And how
was I to know, pray, he would play a trick
like this on us?"

"We'll soon put paid to such tricks,"
said Rory Dubh, coming to look over the
parapet again. "We'll lock him up in the
schoolhouse once those policemen catch
him!"

He pointed toward the policemen who
were now running toward the Bodach from
both sides of the glen, and all along the line
of the parapet Donald saw heads being
craned to watch the arrest being made. On
the mountainside, too, people were pointing out this excitement to one another, and
some of them were rising to their feet to get
a better view of the Bodach, for the floor

79

of the glen was very uneven and there were also great clumps of gorse and rocky outcrops that hid him from some of the watchers.

The Bodach himself did not seem at all concerned by the sight of the policemen advancing on him. He had turned away from the dam by this time and, like a man taking a peaceful Sunday stroll, was wandering slowly up the glen. He crossed over a little ridge of ground that hid him from the view of the people on the dam, but the policemen were only seconds behind him, and everyone waited, expecting to see him being dragged back across the ridge.

To their surprise, however, the policemen were empty-handed when they reappeared on the ridge a few moments later. Questions ran like wind through grain among the ranks of all the people watching, then the muttering sound of questions swelled suddenly to shouts of astonishment as first one person, then another, and finally the whole great throng of people, saw the Bodach again.

He was nowhere near the ridge this

time—in fact, he was on the farther bank of the river, a good two hundred yards away from the ridge. Yet it was only a matter of seconds since he had disappeared behind this, and no one had seen him move from there to his new position.

"How on earth did he manage that!" Rory Dubh exploded.

"The same way as he got away from Constable MacDonald in the first place—by magic, I suppose," Callum Mor said with a sarcastic sort of smile, but Rory Dubh was in no mood for joking.

"Get down there with your tigers and help to catch him," he ordered. "This is no time to be standing here talking nonsense."

"Yes, sir. No, sir," said Callum Mor, and went off looking like a big dog that had been kicked.

Donald, however, was not so sure that Callum Mor had been talking nonsense, for he had noticed something about the Bodach by this time and it was the same thing that had puzzled him the day he had been caught in mist on the mountaintop. The Bodach was not carrying his staff, and once again this was giving Donald the strange feeling that it was not really the Bodach himself he was seeing but someone who looked in every way like the Bodach.

For a moment he wondered if he should mention this to anyone, but decided against it. They would only say he was talking non-sense, too, he thought, and turned his at-tention back to the chase still going on at the foot of the dam.

The policemen were having no better luck with their next attempt to capture the Bodach, although for a few moments it seemed that they had him pinned in the cen-ter of a great patch of gorse bushes. Yet when they rushed the bushes at last, there was no sign of him there, and as they came out again, arguing furiously with one an-other, there was the Bodach again sitting on a rock at the riverside, as calm and uncon-cerned as if there were no one in the glen but himself.

Once again the policemen spread out to surround him. Yet once again they closed their net with nothing in it, for the Bodach strolled off behind another rock just before they rushed down on him; and when they saw him again he was back at the foot of the dam, hundreds of yards away from them. Yet still no one had seen him move from one position to the other, and still no one could understand how he had been able to get so quickly from place to place.

He was like a marsh light, Donald thought, appearing and vanishing among the rocks and bushes and ridges on the floor of the glen the way the blue flame of the marsh flickers in and out at night—one moment seen, and gone again the next; one moment near enough for the policemen to reach out and grasp, the next moment as far from them as at the start of the chase.

He turned to Rory Ban, meaning to say something about this, but before he could speak Rory Ruadh said, "You see what's happening, Rory Dubh. Supposing they never catch him?"

"They will—they must!" Rory Dubh exclaimed, but Donald noticed that he went very pale when Rory Ruadh insisted, "Be sensible, man. The Bodach has made it quite plain that he can keep playing this disappearing trick all day if he cares to do so. And if he can do it for one day, he can do it for another, and another, and another. Surely you see what that means!"

"I see all right," said Rory Dubh, beginning to breathe hard. "I see he is taking this way of showing that we cannot catch him, and if that is the case, we cannot make him leave the glen. But if he does not leave the glen, he will be drowned once the level of the floodwater rises high enough."

Rory Ban said quietly, "Then what he said was true. You cannot flood the glen until he gives you leave to do so."

"Nonsense!" roared Rory Dubh, suddenly losing his temper. "I *will* flood this glen, I tell you! And I will do it today— within twenty minutes, when Royalty arrives to press that golden switch!"

"What!" exclaimed Rory Ban. "And take the chance of an old man's death on your conscience! You would not dare, Rory Dubh."

"I am in charge of this program," shouted Rory Dubh, "and there is no one will tell me what I dare or dare not do."

Quite beside himself with rage now, he turned to Rory Ruadh and ordered, "Get along to the powerhouse and tell the engineers we will go on with the flooding, Bodach or no Bodach. Tell them to stand by for the signal from the control cabin."

Rory Ruadh began to protest at this but got such a glare in reply that the words died on him; and so, with a shrug of his shoulders and a look at Rory Ban that said, *What can I do?*, he hurried off to the powerhouse.

Rory Dubh moved away to explain the situation to the Lord Lieutenant, for still the uproar over the Bodach was growing. Down below, the Chief Constable himself was using a megaphone to shout directions for the hunt, and every time the Bodach slipped through the policemen's fingers all the watching people roared as loud as a crowd at a football match. Up on the dam itself the Town Councillors were all making speeches to one another about the disgrace of such a hitch to the proceedings, and the Lord Lieutenant looked fit to burst with annoyance over the whole affair.

Rory Ban and the Campbell family

looked at one another, the only silent ones in the midst of all this noise.

Donald saw that his mother had gone even paler than Rory Dubh before he lost his temper, and the faces of Rory Ban and his father were set hard as rock. He waited for one of them to speak; and when the minutes went by without a word from any of them, he asked anxiously, "Will Rory Dubh drown the Bodach? Will he?"

"Not if I can help it," Rory Ban said grimly. "Not if I have to go on bended knee to Royalty to beg her not to press that switch."

Donald drew a breath of relief, imagining Rory Ban kneeling to make this plea, and thinking that surely Royalty could not refuse to listen to such a handsome young man going on bended knee before her.

"I'll throw Rory Dubh over his own dam before I let him harm the Bodach," Ian Campbell growled, with a fierceness that Donald had never heard in his voice before, and then suddenly his mother said, "You'd better decide quick, then, what it's to be. Here comes the royal car now!"

Donald rushed to the far side of the parapet and saw a car drawing up at the schoolhouse. It was the longest and sleekest and blackest of all the cars yet to arrive, and there was a red-and-gold pennant fluttering at the front of its hood. A policeman stepped forward to open the door of the car. The band struck up the National Anthem, and from the car stepped a small figure dressed all in blue, with a bouquet of flowers in one white-gloved hand and the other raised to wave graciously to the crowd.

That was all that Donald had time to see of Royalty's arrival, for Rory Ruadh came running back along the top of the dam just then. His face was red with the excitement of the news he carried, and when he reached them he was not slow to tell what it was.

"The engineers in the powerhouse have had a meeting," he panted out to Rory Dubh. "They have decided they will not be a party to the risk of drowning the Bodach, and they told me they will go on strike if you try to flood the glen before the Bodach agrees to leave it."

Rory Dubh stared at this, stared like a man who sees a nightmare coming true in broad daylight. "I have no choice in the matter, then," he said at last. "I cannot flood the glen today."

"That's the way it seems," agreed Rory Ruadh, and he gave a worried look down toward the small figure of Royalty mounting slowly up the steps of the dam.

Rory Dubh followed his look, and in a voice that was bitter with anger and disappointment, he said, "And I will have to cancel the ceremony!"

Rory Ban stepped forward, smiling with relief at the way things had turned out. "Ach, it's not so bad as that," he consoled Rory Dubh. "Let the ceremony go on, and let Royalty make the big speech just before she pushes the golden switch to close the sluice gates. Then, when everybody in the control cabin is smiling and congratulating everybody else, just you quietly push the golden switch back the opposite way, so that the sluice gates will open again. The water level will only have time to rise a little

bit if you do that, and so you will both save
the Bodach and save your face in front of
Royalty."

"Will the powerhouse engineers agree to
that?" Rory Dubh asked.

"Aye, I'm sure they will," Rory Ruadh
answered. "They're reasonable men."

"Then tell them about it while I call off
the hunt for the Bodach," Rory Dubh ordered. "And tell them also that they can
hold meetings and make decisions till they
are blue in the face with talking, but I will
still flood this glen tomorrow, or my name
is not Rory Dubh Mackenzie!"

With that, he hurried into the control
cabin, looking his old, determined self
again, while Rory Ruadh went quickly back
to the powerhouse. The Campbells and
Rory Ban smiled at one another before they
turned to watch Rory Ruadh hurrying past
the royal procession now advancing slowly
toward them across the top of the dam.

"You heard all that?" Rory Ban whispered exultantly to Donald as they stared
together at the procession.

"Aye, I heard," said Donald, and that was all he did say, although it was far from being all he was thinking.

He would find out the secret of the disappearing trick from the Bodach himself, Donald was deciding. And he would do it soon—the very next day, in fact—for now he was sure there was magic concerned in it somewhere, and he could not wait to find out what that magic was!

6.

THE CO-WALKER

OW, IT WAS one thing for Rory Dubh to say he would flood the glen the next morning but quite another thing for him to do it—even though there was not a sign of the Bodach to stop him this time—for that morning, of course, was a Sunday, and there is no Highlander will break the Fourth Commandment by working on Sunday, which is the Lord's Day.

So that was that, as well the Bodach knew it would be, and one more day was lost to Rory Dubh. Nor did he have any better luck on Monday morning, since the engineers held fast to their threat of a strike if he did not see to the Bodach's safety before he flooded the glen. But long before that time, in any case, his temper had cooled sufficiently to let him see that the engineers were in the right.

From that moment forward, then, Rory Dubh began to use every method he could think of to get the Bodach out of the glen. And from that moment forward there was a perfect procession of people beating a path to the door of the Bodach's house— for that was where they found him, of course, when all the fuss was over; just sitting quietly by his own fireside, as if nothing at all had happened to put so many people in an uproar over him.

The first people to visit him there were a Welfare Officer and the District Nurse, and they looked around the Bodach's but-and-ben, shaking their heads at what they saw.

"Animals in the kitchen," said the Welfare Officer, turning up his nose at a litter of fox cubs bedded down among straw in a corner.

"And no running water," sniffed the

District Nurse, pointing to a pail of water the Bodach had just drawn from the river.

"Who cooks your food for you?" she asked the Bodach. "Who washes your clothes, and who takes care of you when you are sick?"

"I cook and wash for myself, and I am never sick," the Bodach told her. "And what right have you to be putting me through all these questions?"

"We have had a report about you from Rory Dubh Mackenzie," snapped the District Nurse, "and it is my job to look into such reports."

"Quite right," chimed in the Welfare Officer. "And now that we can see the terrible way you live, it is a shame and a disgrace it was not reported to us before."

Then he told the Bodach that he was going to fill in a form saying that the Bodach was In Need of Care and Attention, and presently an ambulance would come to take him to an Old People's Home in the town, where there would be a cook to cook his food and nurses to look after him.

The Bodach said nothing to this, but he

smiled in his beard as the two of them went off down the glen; and later on, when the ambulance men came with their stretchers, he was two miles away up the mountainside, leaning on his staff and laughing as they hunted around for him.

The next person to visit the Bodach was a Security Officer, a big man wearing big black boots and a mackintosh, with his hat pulled well down to hide the cold gray eyes in his hard face. This Security Officer questioned the Bodach upside down and inside out about his past life, and his politics, and his views on everything from apples to astronauts. The Bodach answered every single one of his questions in the form of a story, and gradually the Security Officer fell so completely under the spell of his silver tongue that he went away down the glen again with strange dreams lighting his cold eyes, and on his hard face the look of a man who has seen visions.

The Chairman of the County Council came. A whole swarm of officials from the Hydroelectric Board came, and they all lectured the Bodach about the terrible amount of money it was costing the ratepayers to hold up the flooding. Two lawyers came and warned the Bodach that Rory Dubh had applied to the Courts for permission to have him put out of his house. The Sheriff's Officer came and warned the Bodach he would be in Contempt of Court if he resisted a Court Order. The Chief Constable came and said he had a warrant to arrest him for Causing a Public Nuisance.

"If you can catch me," said the Bodach, smiling in his beard again, and that was all he needed to say to make the Chief Constable stamp off in a rage. As for the others, he said nothing to them at all, except to agree that they were all very probably right, but he was sorry not to be able to oblige them.

Not a day of peace did he get, however, from all the officials who kept badgering him, and to crown it all he was hounded by newspapermen who had discovered a curious thing about the photographs they had taken of the police hunt for him at the dam. The policemen themselves could be seen clearly in these photographs, but there was not a single sign of the Bodach in any of them, and the reporters were determined to find out the cause of this mystery.

"Now, how would I know a thing like that?" asked the Bodach, which was a reasonable-enough question, but he asked it with such a twinkle in his eye that the reporters were angry with him.

"You are just pretending not to know," they told him, and many other things they said besides, which were much harsher than that.

The only kind word the Bodach had in all that time, in fact, was from young Donald Campbell, for of course Donald had lost no time in keeping the promise he had made to himself, and he was up at the Bodach's house on the day after the ceremony with the questions tumbling out of him the minute he set foot inside the door.

The Bodach, however, was not to be hurried in his explanation. "Just you sit quietly, now," he told Donald, pushing him down onto a chair by the fire, and then over to his dresser he went and took from its place there the little old book of ancient and secret writings that was one of his three treasured possessions.

"Listen now," said he, sitting down opposite Donald with the book on his knee. "This book has many strange and marvelous things in it besides the thing I am about to read to you. Also, it will be yours someday, for I mean to leave it to you when I die. So listen well, if you wish to understand."

Then the Bodach read from the book. " 'It is known of old time,' " read the Bodach, " 'that every man of the Second Sight hath also in his nature the power to make a being which is a copy of his own appearance. This Copy, or Echo, or Living Picture, of himself is as like to him as a twin brother, and all who see it will swear that it is truly the man himself. It is known of old, also, that this Copy, or Echo, or Living Picture, is under the command of the man of the Second Sight and will do in every way what he wishes it should do. And the name of it is his Co-Walker.' "

"His Co-Walker," the Bodach repeated, glancing up at Donald and smiling to see the astonished look on his face. "So there, in a word now, Donald, you have your explanation."

"You mean," said Donald, "that *you* can make a Co-Walker?"

"Of course," the Bodach told him. "I am a man of the Second Sight, am I not?"

"And that was what you did at the dam yesterday?" Donald went on. "You sent your Co-Walker down to hold up the flooding of the glen, and then just walked quietly away home under cover of all the fuss that was going on?"

"Of course," the Bodach said again; "and that was why the reporters could not photograph me, for the man they saw was not a real man. He was a part of my mind, and no one can photograph my mind!"

"And of course that was why the police could not catch you!" Donald exclaimed, beginning to laugh. "It was not a real man they were chasing!"

"Aye, they might as well have tried to catch their own shadows," the Bodach agreed, laughing, too, as he closed the strange old book, "if only they'd known!"

"But *I* was halfway to guessing it!" Donald boasted. "You didn't have your staff with you, and that was enough to set me wondering. And once before I saw you without your staff, and I thought there was something strange about you that time, too."

"Ah, well, you see," the Bodach told him, "the power to create a Co-Walker does not stretch to cover a man's possessions, and so my Co-Walker must always be seen without my staff. That is the only way of telling him apart from me."

"But how do you make this Co-Walker?" Donald asked curiously.

And the Bodach answered, "That's easy. Just think of your friend Bocca."

"Bocca?" said Donald, surprised. "What has he to do with it?"

"Bocca," the Bodach told him, "is *your* Co-Walker."

Donald stared at him, too astounded for the moment to say so much as a word, and the Bodach went on, "Where did Bocca come from, Donald? You had only to imagine him and he was there beside you—was that not so? Well, you are not the first child to be able to do this, *and you will not be the last,* for the power to create a Co-Walker exists in the minds of many children. But this power fades, of course, as they grow older, and it is only a man of the Second Sight who can keep it for the whole of his life."

"But Bocca was not an image of me," Donald objected, and the Bodach smiled.

"You never really looked at Bocca, did you?" he asked gently. "But that is not so strange, of course, for I've noticed that children very seldom do look one another in the face. They are always too interested in the game in hand for that!"

Still Donald was not convinced. "No one except me ever saw Bocca," he persisted, "and everyone at the dam saw *your* Co-Walker."

"That's true," the Bodach agreed, "but if you had thought deeper and wished harder when you created Bocca, you could have made him clear enough for other people to see, too. The power is there in your mind, Donald."

Somewhat fearfully, then, Donald asked, "But where does it come from, this power? What is it?"

"My goodness, Donald," the Bodach exclaimed, smiling. "You sound as timid as a wee mouse! But there is nothing to be feared of in this, for the power has certainly not harmed me, and it has not harmed you either, so far as I can see. There is magic in it somewhere, of course, but who knows where magic comes from? Magic is just something that happens when everything is right for it to happen. So do not be bothering your head too much with questions like that. Just be content to know that the power is a gift—a strange one, maybe, but still one that has given you the pleasure of Bocca's company when you were lonely and needed a friend."

"*Bocca . . . ,*" Donald murmured. "I wonder how I came to think of that name!"

"*You* didn't think of it," the Bodach told him. "It came into your mind with the power that bred Bocca there, for that is the name of an earth spirit from times so long ago that even the Stone Circle was new when he was old."

"You were going to tell me about the Stone Circle someday," Donald reminded him, and the Bodach agreed.

"Aye, and I think that maybe the time is ripe now for me to do that."

Rising then, he put the little old book back on the dresser and came back to his place opposite Donald. "Do you remember what I said before to you about the stones?" he asked.

"You said that once every hundred years they move from their places," Donald told him. "You said that they dip their heads in the river and then come back to stand fast for another hundred years."

"And they do that," the Bodach added, "to renew the power that is in them—for there is power in these stones. But before I tell you what it is, I will tell you why I stopped Rory Dubh from flooding the glen, for you might as well know the why of it, now that you know how I did it."

"I think I can guess!" Donald exclaimed, but the Bodach held up a hand and said, "See if you have guessed right, then; for in six days' time it will be the first of May, which is the day that was called the feast of Beltane in olden time. And at the dawn of this year's Beltane, the stones are due to walk again."

For a long moment after he said this the Bodach did not speak again, and there was a look of dreaming and of faraway in his faded blue eyes; but at last he said quietly, "This will be a wonderful thing, Donald, and so I could not let them drown the stones before it happened. Moreover, I am old—old, and I have gathered much wisdom in my life. I want to put it to the test before I die."

"How?" asked Donald, wondering. "How can you do that?"

"Come with me to the Stone Circle," said the Bodach, reaching for his staff, "and I will tell you how, after I have told you the story of the Great Stones."

And so Donald went with him to the Stone Circle, and the two of them stood side by side at its center. The Bodach's tall form towered over Donald, but the stones themselves towered still higher—giant-tall shapes of darkness against the gray light of the fading day—and the feeling came into Donald's mind that he was standing in a haunted place. He shivered, and the Bodach laid a hand, warm and gentle and very comforting, on his shoulder.

"Long, long, and long ago were these stones raised," the Bodach said softly then. "And long, long, and long ago, just before the dawn of Beltane every year, the priests of an old faith came to draw power from them, for there is a magic about this circle. The stones themselves are a part of the earth. Their number is thirteen—one for every moon month in a year of the earth's life; and their shape is a circle, which is the shape of the sun. Thus are earth, moon, and sun all brought together in one pattern, which is a thing of power and mystery not to be understood except by these men of olden times. Yet even for them, the power could not work and the mystery was not clear until the first ray of the rising sun struck over the shoulder of Ben Mor there."

The Bodach pointed to the mountain on

the east side of the glen as he said this, and then went on, "This was the magic moment, then, for which the priests had come—thirteen of them, one for each stone. And among these priests were certain chief men, each of whom carried a staff of office in his hand; and it was always the way of things that one of these chief men was a man of the Second Sight, and his staff of office was the same kind of staff as you see in my hand now.

"And so, just before sunrise on Beltane morning, these chief men led the other priests to the center of the Stone Circle, and there they waited for the first ray of sun to strike the stones. And in the moment of that happening, the power of the stones was wakened and the priests drew it to themselves. The mystery also was made clear in that moment, and in the plain light of it the priests found that they knew the answer to every question that has ever been asked."

The Bodach looked down at Donald. "Now," he said, "you know how I mean to put my wisdom to the test. I shall come here on Beltane morning with my staff, as the men of long and long ago came here, and I shall wait for that moment to happen. For I am a man of the Second Sight, and my staff is the staff of office that was carried always by such a man among the priests of the stones."

Donald stared at the staff clutched in the Bodach's strong old hand and thought that he had never seen one so strangely carved or so black in color. With awe in his voice, he said, "I remember when you pointed your staff at the three Rorys, and it seemed to me then that it moved of its own accord in your hand. Is there really such a power in it?"

"Aye, that and more," the Bodach said, and he told Donald of how he had placed his staff at the center of the Stone Circle that very same night, and of how the staff had moved, pointing to each stone in turn, so that he had guessed the doom that was to come upon them all.

Donald looked in wonder at him, and then in greater wonder still at the staff.

"Where did you get such a thing?" he asked.

"It was given to me at the same time as I received my gift of the Second Sight," the Bodach told him. "For you must know, Donald, that a man need not be born with the Second Sight. This power can be gifted to him by one who already possesses it, and the man who passed on the gift of the Second Sight to me, passed on his staff to me also. And so it has been with this staff for many, many generations of men of the Second Sight, right back to those days of long and long ago."

"I do not wonder, then, that I have always been curious about it," Donald said. "And I do not wonder that you want to stop them flooding the glen till Beltane is past, for *I* would dearly like to see the stones walk!"

The Bodach smiled at this. "You have changed your tune," he remarked. "You scoffed at the idea of the stones walking, the first time I mentioned it to you."

"Aye, well," Donald admitted. "But that was before you told me the whole of the story."

A thought struck him then, as he

remembered what the Bodach had told him of the fate of those who had said they would only believe the stones walked if they could see it for themselves, and anxiously he asked, "Would it be dangerous for me to be there?"

"Not now," the Bodach told him. "The danger is only for those who go to watch out of idle curiosity, but now you are ready to show a proper respect for such matters."

"Well, then?" Donald asked. "Can I be there with you?"

The Bodach looked doubtfully at him. "We'll see," he said at last. "I'll think about it and give you an answer when you come up with the groceries on Friday. But meanwhile, you must promise not to mention a single word of all I have told you."

"Not even to Rory Ban?" Donald asked.

"Not even to Rory Ban," the Bodach repeated. "I have waited too long for this moment to take the smallest risk of its being spoiled."

"Very well, then. I promise," Donald told him; and that was all they had time for that day, since Donald had to be early in bed for school the next morning.

And so home he ran, with his mind all in a whirl over the strange things he had learned; but although he was strongly tempted to put the idea of the Co-Walker to the test by thinking of Bocca again, he still did not do so.

In fact, he admitted to himself, he was just a little bit afraid to try, for he was still not quite sure whether he really wanted to be wise in the way the Bodach was wise.

However, he did want to see the stones walk, and as he lay in bed that night waiting for sleep to come he could think of nothing else but their giant-tall shapes standing out there in the darkness of the glen, waiting out the last few days of their hundred years of stillness; patiently and silently waiting for the moment when they could move—waiting, just waiting . . .

7.

THE WASHER AT
THE FORD

FRIDAY EVENING seemed a long time in arriving for Donald after that, but when it came at last he set off in high fettle, with a basket on either arm, as usual, and Nip and Tuck running at his heels.

The day had been a gray and overcast one, however, and now there was a drizzling rain falling. The path by the river was muddy, so that he had to watch his footing, and his first burst of speed was soon brought down to a steady plod. The rain got down inside the collar of his jacket, and clutching the collar around his neck with one hand, he trudged uncomfortably on; but as he neared the stepping-stones over the ford he heard something that distracted his attention from himself.

It seemed to him that it was a sound of singing he could hear, and as he drew near to the ford he made out the form of an old woman kneeling on the opposite bank of the river and splash-splashing away in the water with some white garment she seemed to be washing there.

It was this old woman who was singing some low and almost tuneless mumble as she washed; and straining his ears to follow the rhythm of it, Donald suddenly heard shouting also coming from the opposite bank of the river.

He looked in the direction of the shouts and saw the Bodach hurrying toward the ford, waving his staff and shouting as he came, *"Go back, Donald! Go back!"*

"What's happened? What's the matter?" Donald called, starting to cross over on the stepping-stones and wondering at the same time who on earth the old woman could be and why she was paying no attention to the noise he and the Bodach were making.

On the opposite bank of the river the Bodach was nearly level with the stepping-stones now, and now in an even more urgent voice he was adding something else to his cries of "Go back!" Nip and Tuck had begun barking furiously, however, and they were drowning out the Bodach's words. Donald looked back over his shoulder, calling angrily for them to be quiet, and saw that neither dog had followed him onto the stepping-stones. Instead, they were cringed down on the riverbank, ears flattened, tails between their legs, and eyes rolling in terror.

In bewilderment at this, Donald turned toward the river's opposite bank again. There were only a few yards now between himself and the old washerwoman, and less than that between her and the Bodach.

"There's something wrong with the dogs," he called, and the words were scarcely out of his mouth when the Bodach took one long stride past the old woman and onto the first of the stepping-stones. He was pointing his staff at Donald as he stepped, and it poked against Donald's chest with a force that nearly knocked him off his balance.

Being young and agile, however, Donald managed to save himself with a hop and skip backward onto another stone. As he teetered back on to his balance there, he saw the old woman straighten her bent back and slap her wet washing across the Bodach's legs, and it was the Bodach who overbalanced and went splashing into the river.

Quickly Donald put down his baskets and reached out a hand to him, and as their hands met he said crossly, "It's a good job for you the water is shallow here. But why on earth did you do it? Why *did* you push me?"

"I'll tell you in a minute," the Bodach gasped. "Pull harder, Donald. I am too stiff to rise by myself."

With both hands and all his strength, Donald pulled. The Bodach came, panting, to his feet, and carefully Donald steadied his passage back to the riverbank before he returned to pick up his baskets again. It was only at this moment that he noticed the old washerwoman was no longer there, and staring round to see what had become of her he exclaimed, "Where is she?"

"Gone where she came from," the Bodach answered. "Her work is done."

"What work?" Donald asked, coming back to the bank with the baskets. "And who was she, anyway?"

"She was the *Bean nighe,* the Washer at the Ford," the Bodach told him. "And I wish, oh, how I wish, Donald, that I had warned you about her before this!"

A sudden chill ran over Donald at these words. He remembered how the dogs had cringed back from following him onto the stepping-stones, and fearfully he asked, "Does that mean she is one of the creatures of the—of the Otherworld?"

The Bodach nodded. "She appears at the ford when there is a life due to be claimed from the glen," he said quietly. "It is a shroud—the dress of the dead—that she washes then, and anyone who sees her must give her a wide berth or she will slap the shroud across his legs, and that means he will be the one who must die."

The hair rose on the back of Donald's neck at this, and then, finding his voice again, he managed to ask, "Would she have slapped it across *my* legs?"

Once again the Bodach nodded. "That was why I had to push you out of her way when the dogs drowned out the warning I was shouting," he said. "A life is what she comes for, and it does not matter to her which one she takes."

"So now," Donald whispered, "now *you* must die!"

"Yes," said the Bodach, and there was a small and terrible silence between them, for Donald found he could not speak again without the words choking in his throat.

"Will it be soon?" he managed at last.

"I do not know," the Bodach answered. "No one can ever tell how much time he has left once the Washer at the Ford has touched him with a shroud, but she does not usually wait to claim her victims."

He looked with pity at the grief on Donald's face and added kindly, "But it is much better that she should take an old life than a young one, Donald, and so you are not to let this grieve you."

"How can I help grieving?" asked Donald, still nearly choking with the misery that was on him. "It seems such a terrible thing that you should have to die to save me."

"Ach, no," said the Bodach, "that is the wrong way to think of it. There is a saying in the Highlands, Donald, that when an old person dies, he is going at last to his own herd. That just means that he is going home to the One that created him, and that is how it will be for me when I die. I have lived a long life and a full one, and now I am ready to go to my own herd."

This was a comfort, in a way, to Donald, and when the Bodach saw him looking a bit less tragic, he went on, "I am sad now only for one thing: that it may happen before I can see the stones walk. Yet even that would not matter, if you would promise me something in return for your life."

"Anything!" Donald exclaimed. "Just tell me what it is."

"It is quite a big thing," the Bodach warned him, but Donald only repeated his cry of *"Anything!"*, and so the Bodach told him, "If I am to die before I can see the Stones move, I want *you* to stop Rory Dubh flooding the glen until the morning of Beltane is over."

Donald stared in surprise at this. He opened his mouth to say, *How can I stop him?* but the question was never asked, for suddenly he remembered about Bocca being his Co-Walker and understood what the Bodach meant him to do.

"But I might not be able to make Bocca clear enough for Rory Dubh and the others to see," he said uneasily.

"You will, Donald. I promise you that," the Bodach told him. "So will you do this for me—will you send Bocca out, as I sent my Co-Walker?"

"I'll try," Donald promised. "I'll try hard. But you will have to tell me what I must do with Bocca once I have made him appear at the dam."

"Think of him dodging capture in the

same way as you would yourself," said the Bodach, "and he will do just that. And remember, it will make no difference whether or not you are at the dam to see this happen, for Bocca is a part of your own mind, and he will always act as you would yourself, even if you are not there to watch him."

"I'll remember," Donald told him. "But if you are not to be here anyway, why do you still want to stop the flooding?"

"Because," said the Bodach, "I want the stones to be given a chance, at least, to walk; and if I cannot be there myself when it happens, I want *someone* to be able to see and mark such a wonder—*you*, in fact, Donald. I want you to be at the Stone Circle just before sunrise the day after tomorrow, on the morning of Beltane."

Donald's heart was already beating faster with excitement at the very thought of this. "Aye, I'll do that for you," he said breathlessly. "I would still dearly like to see the stones walk."

The Bodach smiled a little at the look that was on Donald's face. "Then it looks as if you will get your wish, whatever hap-

pens," he remarked, "for I had already decided to take you with me to the Stone
Circle on Beltane morning, and I promise
you I will do so if I am still here then. And
now we had better be taking these baskets
up to my house."

He bent to pick up one of the baskets.
Donald took the other one and whistled in
the dogs, and they set off together for the
Bodach's house. Nip and Tuck followed un-
willingly at Donald's command, their fright
still showing in the way they slunk along
with their tails well down; but Donald was
far more concerned about the Bodach than
he was about the dogs, for the Bodach's
clothes were wet both from the rain and from
the drenching he had taken when he fell into
the river, and he was shivering badly.

"You need a cup of hot tea inside you,"
Donald told him, and as soon as they got
to the house he put the kettle on and made
the tea. The Bodach changed out of his wet
clothes while Donald was busy at this, and
then the Bodach sat in front of the fire,
holding his cup of tea between his hands to
warm them.

"That's better," he said with a sigh of relief, but Donald noticed that his hands were still shaking and there was still the bluish sheen of cold on the skin stretched tight over his fine, big beak of a nose. Leaning forward, he poked up the fire. The Bodach sat looking into the red heart of it, and after a time he said, "You know, Donald, there are many other Stone Circles besides the one in our glen, but the same story belongs to all of them, and it contents my heart to think that I have told you of it at last. For now I know that at least a little of the wisdom I have gathered will live on after my life is finished, and perhaps you in your turn will also pass on the same story about another Stone Circle. And so the magic will be kept alive, and the wonder at this will stay in men's minds—maybe forever! Would that not be a rare and strange thing?"

"Aye," Donald agreed. "It would and all."

Dreamily he, too, stared into the fire and saw, like an enchanted picture growing slowly before his eyes, the shapes of old mysteries and future magic mingling within the red heart of it.

Neither of them spoke again for a long while after that, but at last the Bodach roused himself. Rising, he took Donald's empty cup from him and put it down on the table along with his own, then he turned back toward the fire and said, "I have one more thing to tell you, Donald, and I must tell it now, even though I had not meant to speak of it until you were older. For now my time may be short."

Donald looked up at him, wondering what was coming next; and laying a hand gently on his shoulder, the Bodach went on, "I have told you that it lies within my power to pass on the gift of the Second Sight, Donald, and the person I have chosen to receive this gift is yourself."

Now, to say that Donald was taken by surprise at this would be putting it very mildly; but this feeling, nevertheless, was all over in a flash, for right on top of it he remembered something Rory Ban had said to him and realized that he should have been expecting the Bodach to talk in this way.

You are like master and pupil. . . . That was what Rory Ban had said of himself and the Bodach—*he the master of a strange wisdom, and you the willing student of that wisdom.*

And that had been true enough—as he had admitted at the time, thought Donald, staring up at the Bodach. Moreover, he had enjoyed listening to all that the Bodach's stories had to teach him. But this was different. This was something that called on him to make a decision about the one thing on which he had never been certain. And he still did not know what to do about it!

"What troubles you, Donald?" the Bodach asked, and his kind, faded blue eyes searched Donald's face as if trying to read the thoughts behind it.

"I'm just not sure how to answer you, that's all," Donald told him. "I'm just not sure that I really want to be wise in the way that you are wise."

"Then let me help you to make up your mind," the Bodach said gently. "We are two of a kind, you and I, Donald; for, like me, you can feel the presence of the Otherworld that lies always in and around and beyond this ordinary world. Like me, you were born to listen for the sound beyond silence and the vision beyond sight which belong to that Otherworld. And so, like me, you will always be searching for these things, and your true happiness will lie in the search and the wisdom to pursue it—the wisdom that only I can give you."

Learn all that you can from him. . . . That was the advice Rory Ban had given him about the Bodach, Donald thought. *His teaching is good because his heart is good.* . . . That was another thing Rory Ban had said about the Bodach. And looking steadfastly into the old and faded eyes still fixed on his own, Donald saw the truth that was in them, as well as the kindness, and knew suddenly beyond doubt that Rory Ban had given him good advice that day.

"Tell me, then, man of the Second Sight," he whispered, "how will this gift come to me?"

"Rise up," the Bodach told him.

Donald rose from his seat and watched while the Bodach took the coiled rope of cow hair from the nail in the wall where it had hung ever since he could remember.

"Face me, and stand close to me," the Bodach ordered, and Donald obeyed.

The Bodach passed one end of the rope around Donald's waist. The rest of the rope he wound in a spiral around his own body from his shoulders to his waist, then gave the two loose ends to Donald to hold.

"Now, your left foot must be placed under my right foot," the Bodach said, "and you must look over my right shoulder."

Donald advanced his left foot a little and looked over the Bodach's right shoulder. He felt the Bodach's right foot come gently but firmly to rest over his own left one, and from the corner of his eye saw him reach out to the dresser beside them to pick up his little book of secret writings. The next instant he felt the Bodach's left hand placed on his head and heard the Bodach begin to read from his book, but he could not make sense of the words, for a sudden dizziness came over him and there was a sound in his ears like the roaring of a great waterfall.

I am going to fall! he thought in terror, and clutched hard at the two ends of the rope that bound him to the Bodach; but he did not fall, and through the roaring in his ears he heard the Bodach saying in a calm and quiet voice, "Comfort you, boy. There is nothing to fear if you trust me."

"I trust you," Donald managed to say, and because that was a true word his fear left him and there was no more roaring in his ears and no more dizziness. The Bodach went on reading from his book, and Donald listened, gazing steadily over the Bodach's right shoulder the while. For a short time only, the Bodach read, but in that short time Donald learned many things that are among the oldest secrets on earth, although they were new and strange to him then. Yet still he found it easy to understand the mystery of all these things, for there was a tingling in his scalp where the Bodach's fingers rested on his head, and this tingling was like the outward sign of a current of power that seemed to be flowing into his mind and lighting up strange treasures of knowledge he had never known were there.

So the Bodach's mind was linked to Donald's mind for the length of time that they were bound together by the rope of cow hair, and so the gift of the Second Sight was passed from one to the other.

"Take the book now," the Bodach said when he had finished reading. "It is yours, along with the gift I have just passed to you. Read it well, and you will learn more from it the more you grow in years and in experience of your gift. Take the rope, also, and keep both the rope and the book safe, against the day when you shall decide, in your turn, who is to receive the Second Sight from you."

Donald took the little book carefully in his hands. The Bodach unwound the rope that had tied them together and coiled it up again, then gave this to him also.

"Look well after these things," he told Donald. "They are the last of their kind in the world, and now you are their sole guardian."

Donald put the book in one pocket of his jacket and the rope in the other, and while he was doing this a question came into his mind. Looking up at the Bodach again, he asked, "Will I tell my father and mother of this?"

"You will not need to tell them," said the Bodach calmly, "for it is not a gift that can be hidden—although you yourself will never know the day or the hour when the power of it will come upon you. That is not something that is within the control of men of the Second Sight. But always, you will find, it will come to warn you of any danger or trouble that threatens you or yours. You will see these things suddenly in a vision, as I saw my vision of the three Rorys. You will speak aloud of this vision, and although the meaning of what you say may not always be clear to those who hear you, they will understand once they see that vision coming to pass—as you yourself understood about the three Rorys. Then your parents will know that you have this gift."

"But they will also want to know how I came by it," Donald pointed out, and the Bodach said, "Very well, then. You may tell them that I passed it on to you. But one thing you must not tell them or anyone else is the secret of the way in which the gift of the Second Sight is passed from one to another. That you may tell only to the one who is to receive the gift from you. And now I must see you on your way, for we have had enough excitement for one day and I am tired."

Indeed he did look tired, Donald thought, seeing how pinched the lines of his face had become and how he had begun to shiver again; and he stretched out his hand to stop the Bodach reaching for his staff.

"No," he exclaimed, "there is no need to come with me. You would be much better to rest now."

"Aye, well," the Bodach admitted. "I've had a trying week, right enough. I could do with a rest now. But go carefully if you must go alone, lad, for all my hopes are pinned on you if the Washer at the Ford should claim me before the morning of Beltane."

"Ach, she'll not come that quick for you," Donald consoled him. "There's only one more day to Beltane now, after all, and surely she'll let you have that little time."

"Maybe," the Bodach said. "Maybe. But if she does not, Donald, and if you have to go alone to the Stone Circle, take my staff with you and wait with it in the center of the circle for the moment of sunrise. The staff will be your own after that, together with the rope and the book, and I think I could not have left my treasures in better hands."

"I'll not fail you," Donald promised, and the Bodach smiled at him. Donald tried to smile in reply, but somehow the moment had so much of the feeling of parting in it that he could not quite manage to return the smile.

So it happened that he was not really surprised the next morning when he learned that the Bodach had been taken desperately ill and that an ambulance had been sent for to take him away to the hospital in the town. And sadly, when he heard this news, Donald remembered how he and the Bodach had taken leave of one another, and realized that this truly had been the moment of parting for them then.

8.

DONALD AND
THE DAM

T WAS A POLICEMAN who brought word of the Bodach's illness to the village, and the way of it was this.

Rory Dubh, it seemed, had at last managed to get a Court Order that gave the Bodach notice to leave his house immediately, and he had arranged to have this delivered by the Sheriff's Officer. Also, to make sure that the Bodach had no chance of disobeying the order, he had asked the Sheriff's Officer to take three policemen with him, and to be at the Bodach's house in the very early hours of that morning. Thus it happened that the Sheriff's Officer and the policemen arrived there, hoping to find him in bed and still asleep; and instead they found him in bed, all right, but wide awake and shivering in the grip of a high fever.

The Sheriff's Officer was not a harsh man, although it was his duty to enforce the law. He saw at a glance that there was no time to be lost in getting the Bodach to the hospital, and instantly sent one of the policemen running back to the village to phone for an ambulance while he helped the other two to make a stretcher on which the Bodach could be carried down the glen.

So it was that early on that Saturday morning a policeman came pounding on the door of Kenny the Shop—who was also Kenny the Post Office, of course. When Kenny woke up and learned the cause of the pounding, he went straightaway to the little switchboard behind the counter of his shop; and sitting there in his pajamas, with his postman's hat on his bald head and his wizened-apple face red with excitement, he phoned the police station in the town. The police station phoned the hospital, and by the time the Sheriff's Officer and the other policemen came carrying the Bodach into the village, the ambulance from the hospital had arrived to meet them.

By that time, too, of course, the whole village knew what had happened, for Kenny had an Ayrshire cow that gave a wonderful lot of milk, which meant that he was also Kenny the Milk as well as Kenny the Shop and Kenny the Post. With every pint of milk he delivered that morning, therefore, he told the dramatic story of the policeman pounding on his door, and himself rushing to the switchboard to phone the police station, just the way it happens in the stories on television.

"And what is wrong with the Bodach at all?" everyone asked him, they being anxious for more news to pass on; and not liking to admit he didn't know this, Kenny said to some, "Och, it's a fever he has." To others he said, "It was a heart attack he took," and to still more inquiries he answered, "It's his lungs," or, "his kidneys"—anything at all, in fact, just to make it sound as if he knew everything.

A terrible man to make himself important was Kenny the Shop, yet still and all it seemed a very sad thing to everyone that the Bodach's life should maybe be nearing its end at last. One after another they remembered the long years of it, and the high respect they had always felt for his wisdom and the gentleness that was in his nature; and the upshot of all this thinking was that everyone turned out to see the ambulance arrive and the Bodach leave the glen—everyone, that is, except Ian Campbell and Rory Ban, for as soon as Ian Campbell heard the news he had set off to see if there was anything he could do to help the Bodach, and Rory Ban had followed with the same intention.

Rory Ruadh was there with the rest, however, his cheerful face looking very troubled for once. Rory Dubh stood alongside him, as stern and tight lipped as usual, but with an uneasy look in his eyes, as if he wondered what people were thinking now of his efforts to get rid of the Bodach. And Donald Campbell was there, of course, along with his mother, who was not slow to speak her mind to Rory Dubh when she saw him.

"So you have got the victory over the Bodach at last, Rory Dubh," said she, grimly. "Well, I'm sure I hope you enjoy it— such as it is!"

"You do me no justice, Mrs. Campbell," Rory Dubh answered in a quiet voice. "I do not welcome victory gained in such a way any more than you do."

No one said anything to this, but Rory Ruadh glanced at Donald and gripped his shoulder in sympathy for the look that was on his face then. There was no talk, either, among the people waiting to see the Bodach leave the glen, and in the silence that hung over the village, Donald had the strangest feeling that time itself had stopped till this should happen.

He felt cold then, in spite of the morning sun's brightness, for the feeling of cold was inside himself around about where his stomach was. His mother was weeping now, and he wished that he, too, could weep warm tears; but that was not possible, for there was no warmth of any kind inside him. There was nothing except this cold, empty feeling, as if he had a hollow space where his stomach should be.

The motor ambulance from the hospital arrived, and the ambulance men came out to get their stretcher ready, but still there was not a murmur from anyone—not even from Kenny the Shop's gossiping tongue. The ambulance men looked around the silent, downcast faces of the people, then one of them asked Kenny the Shop, "Has the Bodach died since you phoned, then, Kenny?"

"God forbid!" said Kenny. "We are just waiting for him."

And so the ambulance men waited also, and presently the stretcher party carrying the Bodach came into sight. Slowly and gently they were carrying him, and when they reached the ambulance at last, pity gripped the people like strong hands squeezing their hearts, for the Bodach's eyes were closed. Outside the blanket that covered him, the long white hair of his beard was spread like strands of white silk that moved only very slightly with the quick shallow gasps of his breathing, and the fine strong features of his face were pale and cold looking as marble.

One of the ambulance men bent over him for a minute and then said to the Sheriff's Officer, "It looks as if he has a bad case of pneumonia, sir."

"That's what I thought," the Sheriff's Officer answered. "We found a whole bundle of wet clothes in his kitchen, and it seemed to me that he maybe got chilled after a soaking in yesterday's rain; and with an old person, of course, a chill is often the first step to a serious illness like this."

Donald was near enough the ambulance to hear this conversation. He thought of the Washer at the Ford and wondered what the ambulance men would say if he told them about her; but even if he had wanted to tell them he was not given the chance to do so, for after that they were very brisk about putting the Bodach into the ambulance. A soft thud, and the door was closed behind him. Then in no time at all, it seemed, the ambulance was drawing away, and the Bodach was gone from the glen at last.

"Well," said Rory Ruadh, after a moment or so, "that's that, I suppose."

He cast an uneasy look at Rory Dubh and added, "I'm sorry to see him go, of course, but there is nothing to stop us flooding the glen now, is there?"

"Nothing at all," agreed Rory Dubh, a gleam coming to his eye. "We'll start right away!"

The cold feeling inside Donald vanished with these words. He felt warm suddenly, warm with anger against Rory Dubh, warm with determination to keep his promise to the Bodach; and before anyone could say a word to stop him he began edging away in the direction of the dam. Rory Ban saw him, however, and so did his mother.

"Donald!" she called sharply. "Where are you going?"

"I'm off to play," he told her, still moving away, and she exclaimed, "Play! After what has just happened! You're heartless, boy—heartless!"

Rory Ban said nothing, but he shook his head at this remark and looked after Donald with curiosity in his eyes.

"It's Saturday!" shouted Donald, turning his face away from the question in Rory Ban's eyes. "I get to play on Saturday." Then he turned away altogether and ran full pelt toward the dam.

Swiftly, as he ran, he worked out the best way of keeping his promise to the Bodach, and decided first of all that he would hide himself so that he could watch unseen when he sent Bocca out to do what the Bodach's Co-Walker had done. The best place for that, he thought, would be on the mountain slope overlooking the dam. There were plenty of hollows there where he could lie unseen all day while he watched what was going on in the glen below, and he could easily reach a suitable one before the signal to close the sluices was given; for although Rory Dubh and Rory Ruadh were ahead of him, they were deep in conversation with one another and walking slowly.

Bold as brass, then, Donald ran on past the two Rorys; and they, being used to seeing boys race down to the dam on Saturday mornings, never even glanced at him. At the dam itself he cut away up the mountainside, scrambling as fast up the slope as any four-legged creature could have done, and when he had reached a good height he stopped to look around for a hiding place.

Right away, he found a hollow that suited him perfectly. It was deep, almost grown over with bracken, and rocky, which meant that the floor of it would be dry. A couple of steps and a jump took him into it, and once settled down there he found that it gave him a first-class view of the floor of the glen and of the dam itself.

There were several men standing beside the control cabin, Donald noted then, and although he could not make out who they were, the great height of one gave him a guess at Callum Mor. The sluices were still open, yet still he knew that the signal to close them could not be long delayed now; and so, shutting his eyes tight against the sunlight and closing off his mind to everything else, he thought of Bocca.

He thought of Bocca dressed like himself in a yellow-and-blue-checked shirt and blue jeans. He thought of Bocca with skinny arms like his own, and freckles like his freckles, and short fair hair all rumpled about the way his own hair was always rumpled; and he thought of Bocca standing at the foot of the dam waving his arms about and shouting in the same way that the Bodach's Co-Walker had waved and shouted.

Long and hard he thought of Bocca looking like himself and acting in this way, and when he had this picture of Bocca fixed firmly and clearly in his mind, he opened his eyes and looked down toward the foot of the dam again.

There was someone there now—a boy, a fair-haired boy in blue jeans and a blue-and-yellow-checked shirt.

This was as much as Donald could see from his high point of vantage on the mountain. Yet deep in his bones, somehow he knew that this boy was Bocca and that Bocca's face was his own face, and his whole body began to tremble with excitement, the way a dog trembles when it wants to leap about yet knows it must obey the order to keep still.

Bocca was looking up toward the control cabin and waving his arms about, and now, thought Donald, came the real test. Could the men on top of the dam also see Bocca? Had he made the picture clear enough for that? The Bodach had promised him he would be able to do so. The Bodach had passed on to him the gift of Second Sight that made sure he would have the power to do so. Would the power work?

The tall man he had guessed was Callum Mor leaned over the parapet of the dam. He turned to speak to the men beside him and then pointed down toward the foot of the dam. He shouted something. The other men leaned over the parapet and began shouting also; and with his heart giving a final great leap of triumph, Donald knew that they had all seen Bocca and had been deceived into thinking it was a real boy standing there defying them, as the Bodach had defied them.

It would not be long, he thought, before they tired of shouting orders and turned to action. Then matters would turn out just as they had with the Bodach. The tigers would not be able to get rid of this boy, nor would they be able to catch him; and smiling to himself at the thought of the merry dance he would lead them, Donald waited for the next move in the game. A minute later he saw Callum Mor striding across the floor of the glen toward Bocca.

I'll let him get close, Donald thought; and obedient to the thought, Bocca stood still where he was till Callum Mor was only a step away from him. Callum Mor shot out one huge hand and grabbed, but he grabbed only at the air, for in the same instant Donald thought Bocca a hundred feet away from him. And there *was* Bocca, waving and calling mockingly, that very distance away from Callum Mor.

Shaking his fist, Callum Mor lumbered after him, but Bocca kept dodging ahead just out of his reach, just the way Donald wanted him to do. Callum Mor stopped and blew shrilly on the whistle he always carried with him, and within a few minutes tigers appeared from all over the place to help him in the hunt. Rory Ruadh came with the tigers. He was not wearing his steel helmet, and Donald recognized his flaming red head bobbing up and down among the men trying to corner Bocca.

He grinned at the sight of it, and grinned also to see that there was now only one man left standing on top of the dam. That man, Donald guessed, must be Rory Dubh, still stubbornly awaiting his opportunity to flood the glen; and with his grin growing to a chuckle, he set about inventing new tricks for Bocca to play on his hunters.

He thought Bocca into the middle of the river, so that the tigers got soaking wet plunging in after him. He thought Bocca away from in front of a tiger who was chasing him, and around behind the tiger instead, then in front, then behind, and so on, until the tiger was whirling around and around like a dog chasing its own tail. He thought Bocca suddenly stopping to kneel down in front of a bunch of tigers hot in pursuit of him, so that they tripped over him and were sent sprawling in all directions. But the best trick of all, in Donald's eyes, was when Callum Mor and Rory Ruadh stopped to argue with one another and he thought Bocca popping up between them.

There they were, the two of them, their arms going like windmills as they stood face to face, bawling and shouting at one another, and each very likely blaming the other for everything that was happening. And there Bocca was, suddenly standing between them, and both men were shooting out their hands to grab him; but they only grabbed one another, of course, for Donald thought Bocca away again as quick as a flash.

Yet still it was plain to see that neither Callum Mor nor Rory Ruadh could believe the evidence of their own eyes, and they each held on to the other, each fighting and struggling in the other's clutches and each roaring to the other that he had made a mistake.

Donald laughed at this, laughed until his ribs were sore, but he could not think of any more tricks to play. For a while after that, accordingly, he simply lay and watched Bocca doubling and twisting away out of the tigers' reach, then vanishing when the chase grew too close, only to reappear again in a different place. But that, of course, was all he had ever really needed to do because, since Bocca was just a part of his own mind, it would always be impossible for the tigers to catch him.

Indeed, thought Donald, remembering what the Bodach had told him about Co-Walkers, Bocca would go on dodging capture whether or not he was there himself to watch this happening. He might as well go home for his lunch now—and in fact, that was probably a wise thing to do, for who would believe it was Donald Campbell playing such tricks in the glen if the same Donald Campbell was sitting quietly at home eating his lunch? That was enough to raise another chuckle from him, and feeling highly amused once again and very pleased with himself, he set off home for his lunch.

There was food ready on the table for him when he did get home, for Donald had a good clock in his stomach; but there was something else waiting for him also, and that was a row of angry faces all ready to fling questions at him. There were his father and mother, to begin with, and there was Rory Dubh, all three of them looking as black as thunder. There was also Rory Ban, but Rory Ban's face was not angry. It was a look of curiosity he was wearing, and he did not join in the hullabaloo of questions that greeted Donald's appearance.

Donald let the first rush of these questions go over his head while he spooned up his soup, and then he put a question of his own. Looking at Rory Dubh, he asked, "How can I be sitting here at my lunch at the same time as I am doing all these things you say I am doing at the dam?"

Rory Dubh gave him a look that would have cut cold iron. "You're too clever by half, young Donald," he said grimly, "but now that you *are* here, you'll stay here until I press that switch to close the sluices."

"You don't have to worry about that," Ian Campbell said just as grimly. "Master Donald will not be stirring from this house again until I give him leave to do so."

"Very well," said Rory Dubh, and with a nod and another hard look at Donald, he went away out.

Donald carried on with his lunch, which was very good, being a piece of the chicken his mother had cooked in the soup, along with a baked potato and fresh butter, and leeks in white sauce.

"*Was* it you they were all chasing in the glen this morning, son?" she asked as she sat watching him eat this.

"No," Donald told her truthfully. "It was not me, Mam."

"It looked like you," his father said. "I saw the boy, and he was the spit and image of you."

"Aye, but you see now that it was not Donald," Mrs. Campbell said, before Donald could reply to this. "I told you that at the time, Ian, for I saw him too, remember. And for all that boy was so like Donald, I *know* it was not him. I just know it in my heart, and surely a mother's heart cannot be wrong where her own son is concerned."

Rory Ban said nothing, although his look invited Donald to make some remark on this speech by his mother. Donald knew very well, however, that he could not say anything about the Co-Walker without giving away the whole of the Bodach's secret, and that was something he was determined not to do. At all costs, he had decided, he must keep faith with the Bodach, and so he remained silent.

"And I'll tell you something else," Mrs. Campbell said. "I will have a word to say to that Rory Dubh Mackenzie when he finds he is wrong about Donald, and I just wish he were here now to listen to it!" And she cut a slice of apple pie for Donald with a look on her face that showed she would have liked to take the knife to Rory Dubh instead.

It was only ten minutes after this that she got her wish, but it was more than a word she said to Rory Dubh when he arrived back then with the news that the tigers were still hunting a boy who looked exactly like Donald. The sound of her voice raged like a storm over Donald's head as he ate his apple pie, for there is no one quite so fierce as a mother who thinks her son has been wronged. Rory Dubh shrank away from the force of it, and the storm went on until Donald rose from the table and asked, "Can I go out again, please?"

"Aye, away you go, son," his father answered, with a glower at Rory Dubh that dared him to say otherwise.

"I'll come with you, Donald. I can do with a breath of fresh air," said Rory Ban, and out they went together with no one—least of all, Rory Dubh—raising a finger to stop them.

"And what are you going to do now, Donald?" asked Rory Ban when they were away from the house.

"The same as I've been doing all morning," Donald told him. "I'm going to sit up on the mountainside and watch the hunt for the boy that looks like me."

"And who can play the same disappearing trick as the Bodach played, eh?" Rory Ban remarked. "And who is using this power, as the Bodach did, to hold up the flooding of the glen?"

Donald halted in his tracks and faced Rory Ban squarely. "Rory Ban," he said, "I know a great deal more now than I did at that time, but I cannot tell what I know to anyone—not even to you, for I have promised the Bodach. But this much I can tell you. Tomorrow after sunrise Rory Dubh will be free to flood the glen, and what I am doing today is being done for the Bodach's sake. For soon he will be dead, and I have undertaken to carry out his last wishes for him."

Rory Ban gave Donald look for look as he spoke, and gravely he said in reply, "I said once that the Bodach and you were like master and pupil together, but now it seems to me that you have passed beyond the stage of pupil and are the Bodach's equal in some matters. There is no need, therefore, to tell anything to me or to anyone else, for none of us can follow you along the way the Bodach has guided you. Yet I wish you well, for the Bodach was my friend as well as yours, and it seems to me now that you are doing much for friendship's sake."

With silence between them after that, they walked on up the mountainside together; but their silence was that of people who understand one another too well to need talk, and at Donald's hollow they took friendly leave of one another. Rory Ban climbed on to where his rows of young trees waited for the touch of his green fingers on their growing strength, and Donald took up his watch on the floor of the glen far below him.

Bocca was still there of course, and still playing will-o'-the-wisp with Callum Mor and his tigers, but the pursuit of him had slackened by this time, and it was plain that the tigers were exhausted by all the running back and forth he had caused. Donald smiled to see this, but he knew what a stubborn man Rory Dubh was, and so he guessed that the chase after Bocca would go on till darkness put an end to it.

Patiently, therefore, he settled down to his watch, knowing that Bocca had already succeeded in stopping the flooding of the glen for that day, but well content to wait for the coming of darkness to prove this to Rory Dubh.

9.

THE STONE CIRCLE

HE SOUNDING of the Klaxon horn that Callum Mor used to call his tigers in was Donald's signal that the hunt was over for that day. Cautiously, he let another half hour pass after that, then he shut off the picture of Bocca that he had kept clearly fixed all day in his mind, and that was the end of his Co-Walker for the time being.

He felt tired suddenly, then, and he must have looked tired also, for when he got home and said that he wanted to go early to bed that night, his father and mother agreed this was a good idea. His father was nobody's fool, however, and he looked very keenly at the white face on Donald and the dark smudges under his eyes.

"Playing all day on Saturday has never made you this tired before," he said. "Furthermore, I have the feeling that you know something about the boy who held up the flooding at the dam and who looked so like you."

"So have I," said Donald's mother, who was no fool either, although she had been so quick to defend him against Rory Dubh. "What have you been up to all day, Donald?"

"I have been keeping a promise," Donald told them, and his father said, "Well, there's no harm in that—if the promise itself was a good one. But how are we to judge if that is the case?"

"It was a promise I made to the Bodach," said Donald then, and his voice trembled, for he was remembering his last sight of the Bodach and it made him feel suddenly near to tears.

His father and mother looked at one

another, and his father said gently, "We'll take your word that you were up to no harm, then, Donald, for we know that the Bodach would never ask anything but a good promise from you. Now, away to your bed, and sleep some of the tiredness off you."

"And don't you fret over the Bodach," his mother called after him. "They are clever doctors in that hospital and he will not go to his own herd for a while yet, God willing."

Donald knew differently, however, and it was little sleep he got that night for thinking about what he knew. Besides which, he was afraid of oversleeping and so leaving himself too little time to collect the staff from the Bodach's house before he went to the Stone Circle the next morning.

A light doze from time to time was the best that he could manage, therefore, and at two o'clock by the little clock at his bedside, he rose and dressed in his warmest clothes. Then, taking his shoes in his hand, he crept from his room and out the back door of the house. There he slipped on his shoes and walked quickly and quietly away through the village and onto the track leading to the Bodach's house.

It was a cold night, really cold, and he felt glad of his thick trousers and heavy sweater. The new moon was only a thin slice of yellow in the sky, but still he had no difficulty in seeing the path, for the stars were clear and bright in the cold air. He walked quickly, therefore, and soon reached the ford. There he halted for a moment, looking around to see if there was any sign of the *Bean nighe,* but there was nothing to be seen except the dark shapes of the stepping-stones among the rushing white of the water, and so he crossed over without fear to the other bank of the river.

Past the Stone Circle itself he hurried, thinking how tall and dark the stones looked in the cold starlight, and so on to the Bodach's house. The door of it was unlocked. Donald pushed it gently open and groped his way to the dresser in the kitchen, where he fumbled around until he found a box of matches lying ready to light the lamp that would never burn there again. He struck a match and held up the little flare of it toward the corner where the Bodach had been accustomed to keep his staff.

The match burned down, singeing his fingers, but he had seen the staff leaning in the corner and, stepping toward it, he reached out a hand. His fingers closed around the staff, but the carving on it made it awkward to hold. He shifted his grip a little, and as his hand slipped over the carvings they seemed to move and writhe beneath his fingers like living things.

Just for a moment this made Donald waver in his purpose, but he had a promise to keep to the Bodach and he meant to keep that promise; and so, taking a final firm grip on the staff, he carried it with him out of the Bodach's house and set off on his way back to the Stone Circle.

When he was about twenty yards away from it he stopped to look around for a place where he could wait in comfort for the moment when the stones would move, and found a raised bit of ground that was thickly covered with last year's heather.

The mat of tough, springy stems was just what he needed between himself and the cold damp of the ground, and he sat down on this bank with the staff laid across his knees.

There were still two hours till the actual moment of sunrise, he reckoned, but it should be gray light in about half an hour and this gray light would grow almost into full daylight before the sun itself could be seen rising over the shoulder of the mountain. There was nothing he could do now, therefore, but wait. The previous day had taught him how to do that patiently, and so he leaned back on his heathery bank and stared up at the stars, and waited.

Donald found it very comfortable lying there, and stars are very interesting things if you have time to study them. They made all sorts of strange patterns in the sky, he discovered, and when he had traced these for a while he began to count the stars instead, and managed to get up to 5,092 before the gray light growing in the sky began to dim their brightness. Sitting up then, he realized he had been on the point of dropping off to sleep again, and shook himself briskly wide awake.

It was still very cold, he thought, and there was also a dampness about the chill that was in the air now. Shivering, he hugged his knees up to his chest to try to hold in such little warmth as he had left, and began to work out how long he still had to wait till sunrise. An hour, more or less, he decided, and thought gloomily that it was going to seem a long hour, even though it was almost full light now.

The dampness he could feel in the air came from a white ground mist that was beginning to rise from the floor of the glen and spread all over it like a great blanket of teased-out cotton wool. Over the river it hung like clouds of steam, and it was piled like snow around the foot of the Great Stones. Donald crouched, watching it and wondering how long it would take to clear, but ground mist needs wind to blow it away or sun to suck it up, and there was neither wind nor sun as yet.

Lazily and slowly, very, very slowly, the

mist drifted in the small eddies of air that were there. In thin, thin spirals coiling and spreading at a snail's pace, it drifted upward, growing thinner and thinner as it spread, until the whole glen seemed to be full of a fine, smoky haze. Donald peered through this haze toward the stones and saw that they were no longer firm black outlines against the gray light of the growing day. The mist hung around them now like drifting, flowing garments clothing their tall shapes; and like long white hair drifting and flowing also, it crowned the head of each one.

They were more like tall old men now than stones; old men clothed in drifting white robes that moved slowly as they moved. . . .

With a sharp thrill of terror in his heart, Donald realized the picture they made. He blinked, and stared, and blinked and stared again, his heart beating fit to burst with the excitement and terror that ran through his blood. Were they stones, or were they old men? The drifting mist defeated him, and he could not tell. All he could say for certain was that they were tall shapes in flowing white, *and that they were moving!*

Clothed in mist—or was it more than mist?—they were drifting toward the river through the smoky haze that filled the glen, drifting slowly, a long line of white shapes like tall priests walking in solemn procession toward the trembling, rushing white of the mist-hazed river. And like tall priests bowing before something he could not see, each of them bent as it reached the river, bent right down and dipped its head into the rush of white water.

Then slowly, slowly, each one rejoined the procession drifting back from the river; and in the tense, speechless excitement of his watching, Donald thought of the Bodach's story of the Great Stones. He thought of the priests of the ancient faith who had gathered within the circle, the priests who had made a magic to draw the power of the stones into themselves; and the strange thought came to him that maybe the priests and the stones were one— that the stones themselves were priests who had been frozen into a magic stillness that could only be broken once every hundred years.

Now they were standing again where they had been before he saw them move, but the mist was still clothing them. He still could not tell what they were—priests or stones—and he knew that not for all the promises in the world could he venture into the center of the circle they made. Yet it lacked but a short half hour now to sunrise.

Looking eastward over the mountain, Donald saw the gray sky there taking on a tinge of pink, and yellow light beginning to glow through this pink color. The light shone more strongly through the pink, brightening it to a deep, burning red. The yellow light itself became a brilliant gold, and as the sky shimmered brighter and brighter with these colors, so the mist in the glen began to shimmer, as smoke does when flame is trying to force a way through it.

The haze of it spread wider, rose higher, grew thinner. It rose upward from the stones, drifting higher and higher, rising faster and faster, till Donald could see them outlined dark against the daylight, and unmistakably stones again. He rose to his feet, the staff gripped firmly in his hand, his eyes fixed on the shoulder of the mountain where the rim of the rising sun would appear, and all his courage now gathered up into a huge burning knot inside his stomach.

The stones were only stones again, he told himself. He could safely venture in among them now—and even if he could not venture safely, he would still do so, for the Bodach's sake. The Bodach had the right to know, before he died, that *someone* had taken his place, even if that someone was only a boy feeling lonely and frightened half to death with the strangeness of all he had seen. Donald gritted his teeth and tightened his grip on the staff.

Now! he told himself, and shot forward like a bullet aimed straight for its target at the center of the circle. He was there before he knew it, jerking to a stop as if he had been pulled up short on a rein, with one arm flung up to keep his balance and the staff in his hand thrust out with the gesture.

In that precise instant, also, the first ray of the sun shot over the mountain.

Like a finger of flame it stabbed downward into the center of the Stone Circle, and like flame it ran down the staff upraised in Donald's hand. And the staff twisted in his grip like a live thing writhing in flame. And the shock of the power that was in the staff ran through his hand and his arm and his whole body; and trembling in the shock, he stood with his face upraised to the rising sun pouring down on him from the mountaintop.

His eyes were closed against the strength of its golden glare, but from head to toe he was bathed in it. His body was full of the warmth of the sun. He felt light and lifted up by the power of it, and although his eyes were closed he could see the vision beyond sight and in his ears was the sound beyond silence; for in his mind, too, the golden power was blazing. In its light he could see all the secrets of the Otherworld, and he knew then, as long and long ago the priests of the stones had also known, the answer to every question that has ever been asked.

For a few splendid moments only this lasted, then the staff became still in Donald's hand. He opened his eyes and looked at it, and looked at his knuckles, showing white with the strength of the grip he had kept on it.

"I am the master of the staff now," he said, aloud and clearly; and he knew that this was true, for he had not been afraid to keep his hold on the staff, and so he had not failed the test of the power that was in it.

He looked at the stones, turning himself around so that he could see each one standing still and dark and giant-tall in the bright sunlight.

"I have learned the magic that was made to draw your power from you," he said, aloud and clearly; and he knew that this also was true; for although the great knowledge that had touched him was already beginning to fade from his mind, he knew it was the flame finger of the sun on the staff that had made the magic of his

164

splendid moments. Then Donald looked beyond the stones, and he saw the Bodach.

He was standing quite near the stones, near enough for Donald to see his long white hair and his beard lifting gently in the light breeze that had followed the sun's rising. He was looking toward Donald, as if watching him, but there was a curious stillness about him and he did not move until Donald shouted and began to run toward him. Then the Bodach raised one hand; but he did not call out in reply, and it was not a greeting his hand gave but a wave of farewell.

Puzzled, Donald stopped short in his run and stared while all sorts of questions sprang to his mind. Why had the Bodach not returned his greeting? How had he got out of the hospital? How had he managed to get all the way from the town to the glen? And sick as he was, how had he managed to walk alone from the village to the Stone Circle? Then suddenly he realized that there was one answer to all of his questions.

This was not the Bodach himself he was seeing, but the Bodach's Co-Walker!

Even as this understanding came to him, however, the form of the Co-Walker began to fade, as a shadow fades before the sunlight. Then Donald realized also that the Bodach must have used the last of his strength to send out the Co-Walker, and that now he was dying.

Quickly Donald called out—called again and again, and held up the staff to show that he had kept his promise. The Bodach's Co-Walker nodded as if to say that he understood, and then with a final wave of farewell, he turned and moved away down the glen.

Slowly, slowly, he moved, his silky white hair and beard drifting softly, like thistledown, in the morning's light breeze. Fainter and fainter his shape became in the bright sunlight, till it was only a shadow drifting away across the grass, the last shadow of a gentle old man drifting, drifting gently away. Then finally even the shadow vanished, and Donald knew that the Bodach was dead.

Leaning on the staff, he stared out over the bright, empty space ahead of him.

But the magic is still alive, he thought, and told himself that this was what the Bodach had wanted, and this was what really mattered—that there should always be someone who could pass on the story of the Great Stones, and so keep the magic alive.

So, for a while, Donald stayed. Then he, too, began walking away over the morning green of the grass, and as he walked he thought that there was nothing now to stop Rory Dubh flooding the glen, for now the Bodach had got his wish and so the Bodach's leave was granted. By the evening of the next day there would be nothing but water where the green glen lay around him, and by the evening of the next day the stones would be drowned.

But the Bodach had told him that there were other Stone Circles in other glens, and so not once as he went homeward did Donald look back at the stones that were doomed.

Instead, he looked upward to the mountain, and he thought of the many mountains that rose beyond it and of the glens that lay between the mountains. He thought of the day that would surely come when he would find another Stone Circle in one of these glens; and because he knew that the magic would not die so long as he was alive, and because he was young and the sun was shining, these thoughts began to ease the ache of sorrow that was in his heart for the Bodach.

Thus it was, then, that the Bodach's vision of the Second Sight came true; for the pinecones that Rory Ban planted grew into a forest, the powerhouse of Rory Ruadh brought man-made lightning to the glen, and Rory Dubh brought death by drowning to the glen and to every creature in it. And the Bodach also died.

Yet the stories he told were remembered, the gifts he left were cherished, and the magic was kept alive. And so thus it also was that the Bodach went in peace at last to his own herd, leaving comfort behind him instead of grief, and in the heart of young Donald the strong hope of finding walking stones and sunrise magic again, in some other glen, on some other day.